MURDER OVER THE COLD GRAVE

BLYTHE BAKER

When a serial killer draws Lillian Crawford into a deadly game, she and Eugene Osbourn must team up one final time to thwart their mysterious foe. But will they stop the murderer's twisted game in time to prevent one more death?

1

___

Late autumn had become quite the boisterous time in London, and it had nothing to do with the weather itself. The days grew shorter, but the longer evenings only meant more time for fabulous dinners and parties and every manner of social gatherings. It seemed that every night we weren't at Eugene Osbourn's family home, we were at Cousin Richard's, or perhaps Dorian Yardley's new house that he had acquired recently, as per his inheritance. We had all begun to expect a proposal to Gloria any day, given the way Dorian was getting his life seemingly in some sort of order.

This pleased Richard, who did not seem as worried about a looming empty house as I might have expected. Instead, he seemed to simply be grateful that his eldest daughter was no longer in danger of ending up an old maid. William, he would be content with...and the boy also seemed eager to have full run of the house without his sisters' presence.

It was one such evening, long and comfortable, when

we were gathered around Richard's table. It had become a familiar place, nearly every seat filled now with the young men in our lives. The room hummed with pleasant conversation, and the warm food and drinks filled our bellies until it seemed like they would surely burst.

"More tea, Miss Crawford?" the butler, Hughes, asked, poised beside me with a steady grip on an elegant, silver teapot.

"Well, why not?" I asked, smiling.

"And I already have the coffee brewing for you," he said. "Just as you and Mr. Osbourn like it."

"You are very kind to keep that so well stocked for us, Mr. Hughes," Eugene said, leaning toward us. His arm pressed against my own, and I flushed at his closeness. We were quite public now about our relationship, and he had no fear of making it plain how he felt about me.

"It's my pleasure," Hughes said. "I know it's a little bit of home for you, and we are happy to make those comforts available."

He strode off, carrying the tea to Marie and Oswald beside us.

I looked over at Eugene, unable to resist the chance to steal a quick glance.

When I found his gaze already sweeping over the side of my face, drinking me in, I smiled, and he casually brushed his fingers over the back of my hand.

"Mr. Sansbury, I have been meaning to tell you," Dorian Yardley said, wiping his mouth with one of the embroidered napkins from across the table. "I heard that your business has recently expanded, and wished to offer my congratulations."

"Indeed, I heard the same," Oswald said, also leaning

forward, setting his fork down. "I heard that an entirely new branch office would need to be constructed?"

Richard cleared his throat and swallowed his bite of lamb as he nodded. "Yes, indeed," he said. "Our reputation for reliability has apparently paid off. We might be more expensive than some of our competitors, but we won't charge an exorbitant fee like many of them will once a job is completed. Compensation, they call it. I call it gauging."

"And Father will be the head of the transition team," Gloria said. "He has been promoted."

"Well, then I offer my congratulations once more!" Dorian said with a brief applause. "How wonderful to hear."

"Wonderful news indeed," Oswald said. "My father told me that the expansion will be in Cambridge, yes? Will you then be moving as well, sir?"

"Oh, no, they need me in London still," Richard said. "I am simply going to be directing them and orchestrating the changes once the shift takes place. I did this same job when we expanded the company the first time almost ten years ago."

"Which is why Father is one of the heads of the company now," Marie said, adding to Gloria's sterling descriptions. "And this will make him the head of an entire department!"

"I am very happy for you, sir," Oswald said.

"It's an honor just to be able to speak with you," Dorian added.

I smirked, and leaned over to Eugene, dropping my voice to a whisper. "It's rather adorable, the way they're trying to outdo one another for my cousin's affirmations."

Richard smiled genially, and then looked down the table at Eugene. "And what of you, Mr. Osbourn? Any interesting stories from your concerts as of late?"

Eugene shifted in his chair, not uncomfortably. "Well, I did run into a rather odd fellow at one of the more recent ones. This was at the...Royal Crown Theatre, I believe? He was quite certain he was blind, and had miraculously gained his sight once again as I had. I told him that was remarkable, of course, and asked how long he had been blind. He then proceeded to tell me that he had never lost his sight, and had never been without it. I assured him that he must have mistaken blindness for something else then, but he told me plainly that he was just as I was, and had experienced a miracle." He shook his head. "Soon after, the man's wife came looking for him, and apologized, saying he had been so looking forward to meeting me, and had been so inspired by my recovery, that he had taken to thinking he had been somehow saved from the same trouble. It's hard to understand, but I think he was just hoping to relate to me in some way."

Laughter floated around the table like bubbles in a glass of sherry.

"It's been enjoyable, though. The reception has been very good recently, everyone wanting to see the formerly blind pianist, now cured." Eugene scratched the side of his cheek, glancing at me. "I might have given up playing all together, out of fear that everyone would reject me, call me a liar and a scam artist...if it hadn't been for some keen encouragement by our Miss Crawford."

"You never should have worried about that," I said.

"People were sure to be happy for you, as they have been."

"As they have been," he repeated with a soft chuckle.

"And what of you, Miss Crawford?" Dorian asked. "Had any good cases lately?"

"No, I haven't," I said, setting down my cutlery. "In fact, since I solved the case with Mr. Burton, I have received no letters, and have not heard anything from anyone."

"That's quite a surprise," Dorian said.

"Yes, that is a surprise," Oswald added. "Given the fact that your reputation has been soaring around the city as of late."

"Yes, that is what Gloria tells me, as well," Dorian said. "She told me that just yesterday, the three of you ladies were out shopping, and a complete stranger stopped you and asked if you were the *famous* detective. How did she recognize you?"

"That I still do not understand," I said with a shrug. "I have had people address me by name at parties that Mr. Osbourn has taken me to, and even more who have recognized my name when I have been introduced." My brow furrowed. "It's somewhat bizarre, although I suppose I have had a mention or two in the papers."

"Well, it isn't as if you are unfamiliar with attention in mass," Gloria said. "Your father being who he is."

"No more than you and Marie," I said. "Our fathers are in the same profession."

"You have been recognized by many," Marie said. "Even if it is just when they hear your name."

"How many cases have you solved thus far?" Dorian asked.

I counted quickly in my head. "Seven, I believe."

"That's remarkable," Oswald said, shaking his head.

"And she has given every one of us here peace of mind," Eugene said. "Having helped each of our families, including her own."

I stared around at each of the faces, and realized that to be true. All those closest to me, and those closest to them...

My cheeked flushed scarlet. "I – well, it is what anyone would have done, really," I said. "What I did was neither special nor unexpected."

"It was both of those things," Oswald said. "I don't believe anyone in my family would have even considered looking into Mr. Dossett's death ourselves. We would have left it for the police, and if they couldn't find the truth...well, my murderous sister might very well have done even further damage."

"Yes, and Mr. Burton claimed himself to be one of my brother's closest friends," Dorian said. "He might have gotten away with his actions, too, and continued on as if nothing had ever happened." He suppressed a shiver. "It's horrific to even consider."

"And we may never have found William when he was kidnapped, if it wasn't for you," Richard said, his eyes shining with gratitude.

I thought of my twin brother, Felix, and how he was nearly blamed for a murder that he had not committed. I had to admit to myself that my skills had been of use then, too. "Well...I appreciate all the kind words."

"You will likely never know the appreciation we have for you and for your hard work," Dorian said, raising his glass to me.

Gloria followed suit, as well as the others around the table. Even William, beaming at me, raised his glass of milk, some of which sloshed over the side and dripped onto the sleeve of his shirt.

"To Lillian!" Eugene said, leading the cheer.

"To Lillian!" Everyone echoed, and all took a sip from their glasses in unison.

"Well, *I* for one am quite relieved that the criminal world has been quiet lately," Gloria said as everyone settled their drinks back down onto the table and resumed their meals. "Who enjoys opening the paper and reading about some grizzly murder?"

"Gloria, you never read the paper," William pointed out.

Gloria shot her little brother a look, but could not open her mouth to retort before Richard stepped in as well.

"Quiet like this is never a good sign, in my observation," he said, his expression troubled. "It usually means that either something sinister is taking place, or is about to."

"Oh, Father, you are far too dark and grim," Gloria said. "Can it not just be that people are getting on for once?"

Eugene glanced at Richard.

"That's not always how it works out," Eugene said, and Richard nodded. "Unfortunately, there are too many people out there who enjoy, and thrive on, the pain and destruction of others."

"Yes, they find some way to benefit from other people's suffering," Oswald said, his face souring.

"Or perhaps the police have managed to intercept any

troubles as of late," I said. "Though I realize London is a large city, and there are only so many officers to go around."

"That's true, of course," Dorian said. "But it is worrying, thinking that some underworld leaders could just be biding their time."

I said, "Well, if it makes you feel any better, during my time investigating, I never ran into anyone I could have considered a criminal mastermind. Most, if not all, the crimes were committed against someone the perpetrator knew. There is always a tie to the killer. Stories that there are faceless, nameless groups of criminals pulling strings all over the city are exaggerated."

Dorian didn't seem entirely convinced.

"You would do well not to hold such claims so tightly," Richard said. "There is an underbelly in this city, as there is in New York."

"Maybe," I said. "But the cases I had investigated were all personal, as I believe most murders are."

"Perhaps," Richard said. "But that does not mean there are not those who will go to great lengths, and commit any crime, to gain fame and fortune."

"You always hear that you shouldn't walk down Waterford Street at night, given the unsavory sort that reside there," Marie said with a frown.

"Oh, and don't forget the eastern side of Royal Court," Gloria said with a shudder. "I have heard the deals made in those dark streets would make one's hair curl."

I resisted the urge to roll my eyes. "All I am saying is that I have dealt with many crimes, and have been able to find the root of them all. It is easy to allow one's fears to overwhelm one, and the imagination to run out of control, concocting ridiculous possibilities of evils. I know full well that powerful criminals exist, as does random violence...but I think such instances are few and far between, and most of the crimes we face are caused by the actions of those we know."

"Well...I've certainly seen enough destruction in my life to realize that everyone has a motive, and everyone is selfish to some extent," Richard said. "People are far more willing to do good for someone if they themselves get something out of it." He looked pointedly at me. "Hence the reason you typically have more than one suspect in a murder investigation, yes?"

"It's true," I said. "There are often multiple people who would have been capable of killing the victim."

"Well, let us hope that Lillian never runs into more grotesque evils, and on a larger scale," Eugene said.

"I would have no hope of finding the guilty party, if they were a part of some large, organized crime syndicate," I said. "And I highly doubt I would survive taking on such a task."

Eugene's face paled at the thought.

"I wouldn't worry too much," Richard said. "But it is always good to remain cautious."

"Of course, cousin," I said. "All this is hypothetical, of course. Who knows if I will ever have another case again?"

"Would that disappoint you?" Oswald asked.

I glanced over at him, my brow creasing. "You know, I have never been asked that before," I said. "I suppose I don't know."

Oswald's eyes darted to Eugene for a moment before he returned his gaze to me. "It's just...isn't detective work terribly dangerous? Is it really something that would be wise for you to be doing for any reasonable length of time?"

"Oswald..." Eugene said in a low voice.

"I only ask because I know there are many who care deeply for you," Oswald said. "And continually putting yourself in danger..."

I could feel Eugene shifting in the seat beside me, and I stiffened.

"Those who care for me accept that my work is part of who I am," I said firmly. "I do not take risks for my own amusement, after all, but for the greater good."

"But what would it take for you to stop?" Oswald pressed.

"When I finally feel that I have accomplished my purpose, and helped everyone I need to," I said.

"Well...you've helped everyone here, around this table," Oswald said. "Who else would you – "

"Oswald...thank you," Eugene interrupted. "Not to entirely derail, but wasn't there something you wanted to discuss? Something about the seamstress for the wedding?"

Marie's face lit up, and she turned to look at Oswald, laying a hand on his arm. "He's *right*! How could I have forgotten?"

She proceeded to speak almost faster than I could keep up with, like a chirping songbird.

"I'm sorry," Eugene muttered under his breath, to me. "I didn't expect him to say anything like that."

"It's all right," I relented, laying my hand over his. "I understand that he means well...and it shows me how much you care."

"You aren't displeased?" he asked.

I shook my head. "I was for a moment but, now I think about it, why should I be?"

"Well...you once were, when Felix questioned you about all this," he said. "I have done my best to support your work and to refrain from stepping in and asking you to stop...though I admit I have wished to, at times."

"You worried that it would push me away," I said.

He nodded. "And I *believe* in you. I have seen your abilities. To ask you to stop seems selfish when you have the skill for helping clients in need, including my own relatives. How could I not be grateful for what you and Felix did? How could I ask you to stop doing what I watched you do for my family and me?"

"If you are ever concerned during a case, you must speak your mind," I said. "If we are ever to make something of ourselves, Mr. Osbourn, of you and I together, then you must never fear my wrath...as nasty as it may be."

Eugene smirked. "I have witnessed your fire and survived. I think I am immune to its heat."

"Are you?" I asked, arching a brow, my smile growing. "You think you know me so well, but you have yet to be in the path of my rage when you have taken the last of my favorite pastry. Do you, Mr. Osbourn, know which one that is?"

His smile deepened. "Blueberry. I have no doubts."

I sat back, raising my brows. "Well...perhaps you know me better than I expected. I underestimated you."

He laughed.

"And *you* are quite fond of apple," I said. "Anything

apple, though I have seen you select a mincemeat tart on more than one occasion."

"There is something about those tiny, dried fruits that I simply cannot get enough of," he said.

Marie still carried on about her wedding, which was to happen in two weeks. It had been all she could think of, and rightly so. Oswald sat back and watched, affectionately absorbed in her. I imagined she could have been discussing the difference between white and ivory and he would have enjoyed listening...though it would surely have been up for debate if he had *heard* what she said, or whether he really cared. Being with her was enough for him.

Dorian, likewise, appeared invested in Gloria, who seemed to be debating with Marie about various plans. Not arguing with her decisions or choices, but about timing, and hoping that the seamstress would be there on time the following morning to size her dress, and saying how she would have a word with her otherwise.

"Lillian..." Eugene whispered suddenly to me. "Would you like to go for a walk with me?"

I saw his plate; mostly untouched. "You aren't hungry?" I asked.

"I can eat later," he said. "Let's slip away before it's too cold outside."

"Well...all right," I said. "I will just need my coat – "

The door to the dining room swung open, drawing all our eyes.

Hughes stepped inside, his face looking surprisingly drawn and pale. He clutched a single letter in his outstretched hand, holding it away from him as if it might burst into flame at any moment.

———

2

"Hughes?" Richard asked, silence falling over the room. "Is everything all right?"

Hughes did not look over at Richard. Instead, he shifted his eyes in my direction. "I'm terribly sorry, Miss, but...a frantic young man just delivered this letter."

I eyed the letter as warily as he held it. It seemed unassuming, as letters went. "Who is it from?" I asked.

"I'm afraid I have no idea," Hughes said, walking slowly around the table toward me.

"Well then, who delivered it?" I asked.

"Once again, I do not know the name," Hughes said. He set the envelope down on the table, as gently as if it were made of glass. "I simply answered a knock at the door, only to see a young man standing on the step, looking frightened. He shoved the letter into my hands, and told me a stranger had approached him in the shadows on the outskirts of town, threatening his life if he did not deliver this message. He ran away before I could ask questions."

An eerie stillness passed over the table, everyone's gazes fixed on Hughes.

"And he told me that the letter was for you, Miss Crawford," Hughes said, dipping his head to nod at the letter.

I stared down at it, noting the clearly printed *Miss Crawford* written on the front. Apart from that, there was nothing else but blank paper. Even when I hesitantly picked it up and turned it over, the back had nothing to offer. No seal of any kind, no watermark.

"What could this mean?" Dorian asked.

"I think we all know very well what it means," said Gloria, leaning away from the table, her eyes narrowed to slits. "Whoever gave the boy this letter is no friend of Lillian's."

I moved my thumb to the sealed part of the envelope, ready to open it, when Eugene reached out and laid his hand over mine.

"You don't have to open it," he said.

I blinked at him, staring blankly. "I know," I said. "But what if it – "

"What if it's filled with some sort of poisonous substance?" Gloria snapped. "And you manage to get all of us killed?"

"What if it's a death threat?" Marie asked, eyes widening.

"It could be nothing more than a joke, meant to throw you off," Dorian said. "I've heard that happens to the police all the time."

"It could be any of those things or something entirely different," I said. "But if I don't open it, I will never know."

"You could claim it was never delivered," Oswald said with a shrug.

"Fat lot of good that would do, since Hughes answered the door himself," I said. "And if the young man who delivered it was threatened, then this is something serious. It must be."

"Did this young man seem genuine?" Richard asked, eyes following Hughes around the table.

Hughes nodded. "Indeed, sir. He truly was frightened, and had no intention of staying around to find out what would happen if he disobeyed."

I hesitated, staring at the envelope. So far, it hadn't started eating through the flesh of my fingers, and I took that as a good sign.

"Well...I suppose if you open it, we can still disregard it," Eugene said. "All it would take is a quick flick of the wrist to find its way into the fireplace."

"True," I said.

"Just be careful, Lillian," Richard said. "I do not have a good feeling about this."

Nor did I...but what else could I do?

My hands shook ever so slightly as I peeled open the envelope. At once, a sickly sweet smell wafted from the inside of the envelope, and I tore it away from my face. I threw it down onto the table, and a handful of purple buds rolled out onto the polished wood.

"Is that lavender?" Dorian asked, eyeing the buds with curiosity.

Oswald reached out and picked one up.

"Oswald!" Marie exclaimed. "Don't – "

He rolled the small, purple flower around between his fingers. "It's lavender, all right," he said. "Which makes very little sense."

I picked up the envelope once more and peered inside. Sure enough, I found a handful more of the flowers, which had permeated the paper with their fragrant aroma. I pulled the letter out and unfolded it.

Eugene leaned over my shoulder to read it, as well.

"*To Lillian Crawford, Private Detective,*" I read. "*First of all, I must inform you that I am impressed with your work. I thought you might have given up this little game of yours by now, but you have continued to press on. Congratulations are in order.*

As such, I have decided to present you with a challenge. A game of my own, if you will. I should like to challenge you to discover my identity. This will not be like any game you have played before, but I believe you will be suited for the job."

"Well, that doesn't sound too difficult," William said. "You are good at finding people!"

I went on, my palms growing slick with sweat. "*Besides...*" I read slowly, my heart pounding in my ears. "*...Who else could find a serial killer but a woman with your skills?*"

I looked up at Eugene, whose face was grim.

Marie clasped a hand over her mouth with a gasp.

"A serial killer?" Gloria hissed.

Richard said nothing, simply staring at the letter in my hands and the dreaded news that it brought.

"Is there any more information?" Eugene asked, hesitantly.

I returned my gaze to the letter. "*I do not wish to give*

too much away, not so soon. I will, however, provide you with a basic list of rules.

1 – You may use any tool at your disposal, including going to the police. I do not imagine they will be of great use to you, but I will allow it all the same.

2 – You may not leave London. The game will transpire there, in the city, so there will be no need to leave. Fleeing will not end the game.

3 – You are not allowed to quit until you have solved the case, just like all the others you have taken on. Not that I am giving you much choice, of course. I am certain the incentive will be enough to keep you going.

"Incentive?" Eugene asked. "What does that mean?"

"I have no idea," I said. "It ends with, *'Your first destination is to be St. Peter's Cemetery. There, you will find further instructions to our little game.'*"

"A cemetery?" Dorian asked, glancing at Gloria. "That's rather ominous."

"This whole *thing* is ominous," Gloria said. "Lillian, don't tell me you're going to go through with this?"

I set the letter down. "I...don't know what to think," I said.

"Who is it signed by?" Eugene asked, glancing over my shoulder.

I looked at the bottom of the letter, my heart sinking. "The name scrawled at the bottom is...*Nightmare.*"

A unified chill swept through the room. Nightmare.

"That's an interesting choice for a name," Oswald said.

"Interesting?" Marie said. "It sounds quite theatrical to me. Who would call themselves such a thing?"

"I have no idea," I said. "I have never heard of a Nightmare."

The small hairs at the nape of my neck stood up straight, goosebumps spreading down my arms beneath the sleeves of my dress.

"And this Nightmare claims to be a serial killer?" Dorian asked. He glanced at Richard. "I have never heard of one of those in London."

"Nor I," Richard said darkly. "It's been some time since I have even heard that term thrown around. It's usually left for fiction."

"How seriously can we take this letter?" Oswald asked. "Is it possible this is nothing more than a joke?"

"That's difficult to say," Eugene said. "I don't think it would be wise to dismiss it entirely...at least, not yet."

"No, I don't think it would be," Richard said. "Might I see the letter myself?"

I sent the letter down the table to Richard, who looked at it with a furrowed brow.

"If this person is a killer..." William said, worry clouding his young face. "Then, does that mean...?"

His question hung in the air, and no one seemed all too eager to answer it.

It was a prospect I had not wanted to consider, though the back part of my brain had already begun to chew on it. I decided it best to voice my thoughts...after one thing was taken care of. "Richard, might it be a good time for William to go to bed?"

Richard glanced up from the letter with surprise, his eyes darting down to his son. "That might be wise, yes."

"No!" William said, jumping to his feet.

"William, this sort of conversation is too mature for you," Richard said. "It really would be – "

"You know full well that I am just going to listen through the door," William said, glaring at his father.

Richard regarded him with surprise and mild frustration. "You will do as you're told."

"I have heard all, several times over. You cannot tell me that I am too young to hear this. Not anymore," William said. Then he shifted his wide, blue eyes to me. "You know I'm right, Lillian. You told me I'm a good partner, and that I have helped you to solve some of these cases!"

I stared at him, and found I could not argue. I sighed. "I cannot deny it..." I said. "You have indeed helped me."

"See, Father?" William said, pointing at me. "I can help. I *want* to help."

Richard pursed his lips, gazing at his son as if seeing him for the first time. "When did you grow up?" he murmured, his expression full of sorrow.

"I will leave this to you, Richard," I said. "We can refrain from speaking any further until he leaves, or if you deem it acceptable for him to stay...?"

Richard sighed. "I suppose..." He hesitated. "You have heard a great deal of these cases. I see no reason not to allow you to stay."

William brightened, grinning at his father as he plopped himself back down into his chair.

I glanced around, my eyes falling on the letter once more. "Very well," I said. "I suppose I will bring a question to the table, then. Have there been any recent deaths in town that have seemed strange, or connected somehow? Perhaps I can go into this better prepared than I currently am feeling."

"Not that I can think of," Eugene said. "As we were saying earlier, it has been quiet."

"Or we haven't paid close attention," Dorian said. "It is possible there is a pattern readily visible, but we might not have noticed because we did not know what to look for or what to pay attention to."

"That's a good point," Oswald said, rubbing his chin. "All the information you have been given is that this Nightmare wishes to play a game, a test of your skills... and that he is a serial killer?"

"That, and the particular location of the cemetery," I said. "Apart from all that, we know nothing."

"Well, you certainly should not go alone to that cemetery," Marie said, folding her arms. "What if this is just a trap, and someone is going to be waiting for you there to..." She didn't want to finish her thought, it seemed.

"Then she won't go alone," Eugene said. "I will go with her."

"As should I," Oswald said, brow creasing.

"No," I said, shaking my head. "Oswald, I appreciate the offer, I truly do, as well as your bravery. But you are marrying my cousin in just two weeks. You do not need to put yourself in any sort of danger. She needs you far more than I do."

Marie looked relieved, and Oswald perplexed. But he looked at his bride to be and softened. "Of course," he said, his face hardening. "I think that....is wise. I'm sorry, Marie. I wasn't thinking – "

She shook her head. "No, it's all right. I am glad you were willing to help. You are very brave...but I am also thankful that you see the wisdom in staying out of this for now. At least I know I will still have a husband come the day of the wedding."

"She's right," Richard said. "If Lillian had not protested, I certainly would have."

I looked across the table at Dorian. "And that goes for you, as well. Gloria would never forgive me if anything happened to you."

Dorian frowned. "That I believe. But what will you do?"

"I will manage just fine," I said. "I always have. I am better prepared than this Nightmare is crediting me."

"She could go entirely alone and walk out of it unscathed," Eugene said. "However, I will ensure that she does not have to go alone. It's always better with support."

"It will just be the two of you?" William asked, worry wrinkling his young forehead. "Didn't the letter say you could go to the police?"

"That's true," Dorian said, snapping his fingers. "Perhaps you should go and ask some of them to accompany you, just in case."

I glanced at Richard, and he shrugged. "If you think it wise, I would recommend it."

I shook my head. "No," I said. "A police presence might frighten this person away. I think this is a test, a chance to unravel the sender's identity before anyone comes to harm. Whoever this Nightmare is, he certainly seems to know some things about me, and I need to take the time to know him. Perhaps this will be a meeting. And if it's a game, he specifically asked for me. If he means to play by his own rules, and he seems to have gone to great lengths to establish them, then I can't imagine he is going to do anything to harm me any time soon."

"And what if this person is entirely mad?" Oswald asked.

"Well, then I will likely be walking straight to my death," I said.

Marie looked horrified.

"I realize this could be some elaborate scheme," I said. "I am not a fool, and I will not take this lightly."

"Then why not just ignore the letter all together?" Dorian asked.

I hesitated, wondering for a moment. "I could," I said. "What harm would it do?"

Richard held the letter aloft. "I don't know if it would be wise. Remember the third rule?"

"Right..." I said. "I cannot back out."

"He may not have given you a choice, but you are going to accept it? Just like that?" Dorian asked.

"You heard what Hughes said about that young man who delivered the letter," I said. "And I have witnessed my fair share of wicked deeds done by these murderers. Someone who is capable of killing has no qualms about doing it again, not usually. I would be worried that the young man would be sought out and killed for my negligence. Or perhaps some other victim would be killed as part of this *game*, something I might prevent. I cannot stand for that...not until I know what I am dealing with."

For a few moments, the only sound in the room came from the tick of the clock, and the popping of the logs in the fire.

"What do you think you'll find at the cemetery?" Gloria asked in a low voice.

"I don't know," I said. "But I have my suspicions."

"Which are?" Dorian asked.

I hesitated answering, not wanting to give voice to some of the worries worming their way into my chest. "Well...I imagine that I will find something rather shocking. What that will be, I can only imagine. Nightmare will likely want to make an impression on me, one way or the other."

Marie shivered, shaking her head.

"More than that, though, I think I will find answers, which is why I must go," I said.

"When will you go?" Gloria asked.

I glanced up at the clock. It was just after eight o'clock.

"I imagine the letter meant I should go tonight," I said.

Murmurs of dissent rose from the rest of the family, but I shook my head.

"I don't want Nightmare to think that I have ignored him. He could go after the delivery boy or someone else." I looked over at Eugene, my resolve hardening. "What say you? Shall we ready ourselves?"

"Now, wait one moment," Richard said, standing to his feet, his palms flat on the table. He glared down the length of the table at me. "Have I no say in this matter?"

"What would you wish, cousin?" I asked. "Do you have any insight that you have not voiced yet?"

He searched my face, and his eyes fell. "No," he said. "I just dread the thought of you being in danger *again*."

"I will manage," I said. "As I have before."

He ran his hand through his hair, and sighed, his cheeks puffing out. "Yes, and I believe you will...except every other time, the danger was imminent, and passed quickly. I have not yet allowed you to leave my house to walk straight into the arms of a killer. What would your mother say? What *will* she say if the worst happens?"

I regarded him, and for the first time, I felt the depth of his affection for me. He did not want me to face this. He worried that I would never return, and as if I were his own daughter, he agonized over the idea.

"I will do what I can to return home," I said. "I assure you. And I will be wise and cautious."

"I will bring her home, Richard," Eugene said, his tone certain. "You can rest assured."

Richard nodded at him, and then to me. "Very well," he said, straightening up. "I suppose that is all I can ask for. I hope you find this creature...and bring him to justice."

"You don't have to ask me twice," I said, getting to my feet. "Come on, Eugene. Let's go."

3

"How are you feeling?"

I glanced over at Eugene as the chauffeur, Ronald, pulled the car up to the curb. "You have asked me that three times in the last half hour," I said, though not unkindly.

He gave me a smile, but I could still see the worry in his eyes. "I know. I suppose it's because this time feels different for some reason. It is unsettling that the murderer has given you so much information. It reminds me of a dog being led around by a piece of meat in order to trap it."

"I know how you feel," I said. "Typically, I go into these situations blind, and the culprit does everything he or she can to avoid detection. The fact that someone is playing with my mind is not exactly my idea of an ideal scenario."

Eugene's face hardened, and he shook his head. "I certainly hope this is not as worrisome as I have allowed myself to consider," he said. "Whatever it is that we find here, I hope it's something we will be able to handle. I am concerned we might be in over our heads."

"I am concerned about that, myself," I said in a low voice as Ronald came around back to open the door for us.

We stepped out into the cold, crisp night. The rains had gone, bringing a bitter cold in the past few weeks. It swept over me, biting straight through my cloak and gloves, whipping my face. I squinted against it, staring around as Eugene climbed out to stand beside me.

The cemetery itself was small and quite old. It seemed that this part of the city had been built up around it and no one ever thought it worth moving or changing.

"This is far smaller than the cemetery Felix and I went to, the day he was arrested," I said, wandering toward the rusted, iron gate. I stood on my toes and peered over the crumbling stone wall, but apart from a few stretches of light peeking between the various buildings both situated around the cemetery and across the street, it remained mostly bathed in deep shadow.

"If Nightmare meant to leave something obvious for us to see, then I must be missing it," Eugene said, standing almost a head taller than me, staring into the darkness.

"Miss?" Ronald asked. "Shall I accompany you both?"

I noticed the chauffeur slide his hand into his pocket, almost reflexively.

I tried to swallow, the thought of *three* of us being unable to face whatever it was we were about to find making me shiver. "If you would prefer that to standing by the car at this hour, I would not refuse you," I said.

He nodded, and stepped up beside us.

Eugene tried the gate, and it gave easily. He glanced at me, his brow rising.

"There really is no reason to wait," I said, steeling myself. "I don't believe we will be able to solve anything standing out here."

Eugene nodded, and stepped onto the cobblestone path inside.

"Just one moment – " Ronald turned around and hurried back to the car. I gave Eugene a sidelong glance as Ronald rifled around inside before withdrawing a torch. "There," he said, returning to us and holding it aloft so that its beam shone on the ground before us. "Thought this might be useful."

"Thank you, Ronald," I said, trying not to allow my voice to shake.

We headed through the gate, and the shadows seemed to swallow up the sounds of the surrounding city. It might have been the fear racing through my veins, my head pounding in my ears.

I despised stepping into a situation so entirely unknown to me. I had utterly no idea what to expect, and what we even should be looking for.

A movement out of the corner of my eye made me stop suddenly, Ronald nearly colliding with the back of me. I reached for my sheathed knives in my thigh holster, whipping them out as quickly as I could.

"What is it?" Eugene asked, whirling around.

Ronald stopped, holding the torch high as we waited while a few anxious heartbeats passed. No one jumped out at us. Nothing attacked.

A bush along the path waved in the strong wind

whipping through the dark cemetery, its branches scraping the empty air like jagged fingernails.

"It's only a bush..." I said, my arms falling to my sides, relief washing over me.

"All right," Eugene said, his pistol clutched in his other hand. "I think we need to take a moment to calm ourselves."

"Unfortunately, I do not think I will be able to be calm about *anything* until we find exactly what this is that we are up against," I said.

"What should we be looking for, Miss?" Ronald asked, peering into the shadows.

"I honestly have no idea, Ronald," I said, starting up the path once again. "But I imagine we will know it when we see it."

We certainly did.

We did not have to walk much farther before we managed to find exactly what Nightmare had laid out for me. Once we came around a corner, passing by a long row of graves so old the names had faded...

Ronald gave a startled cry.

A grotesque scene unfolded before us. A large, muscular man lay stretched out on the ground in front of a blank headstone, prostrate with his arms laid across his chest. His hands, clasped tightly together, clutched a bouquet of dead flowers wrapped in red ribbon.

I took a step forward, my eyes narrowing as I studied his chest. After a few of my own heartbeats, I knew the truth. "He's dead," I said, looking at Eugene. "He's not breathing."

"I suspected as much," Eugene said, as he started toward the body.

"He's really dead?" Ronald asked.

I nodded.

"Who is he?" the chauffeur asked as I approached the man.

"I have no idea," I said in a low voice. The silence of the cemetery seemed oppressive, smothering almost, and goosebumps bubbled up on my arms. "The letter did not tell me what we would find, just that we would find *something.*"

The corpse had a rugged, chiseled face, shadowed with very little fat. A long, narrow scar ran from the edge of his eyebrow to his jaw. He wore a thick, mossy green jacket lined with pockets, which almost blended in with the grass beneath him.

"Military, perhaps?" Eugene asked, eyeing the jacket as I did.

"Maybe…" I said.

Ronald hung back, but angled the torch's beam for us to be able to examine the man better. Apart from the scar, his skin appeared untouched. The only odd feature I found was that his eyelids seemed purple, almost as if they'd been stained.

"No wounds or lacerations, no bruises," I said. "No obvious means of death."

"Internal bleeding? Or suffocation?" Eugene guessed. "Or maybe the wound is beneath his clothing?"

I frowned. "I don't believe so. And he looks as if he has not been dead for very long," I said.

Eugene looked up at me. "Then how could Nightmare have written that letter and gotten it to you as quickly as he did?" he asked.

I blanched, and turned away from the dead man. "He must have been killed just a short time ago..."

"The headstone says nothing," Eugene said, his face pale...though I couldn't be sure that wasn't just due to the chill in the air mixed with the light of the torch. "But I doubt that has any bearing on this man or why his death has any part in all this."

Many questions began to rise in my mind, one coming to the forefront of them all. "Is this cemetery of some significance? Or did the murderer just drag this body here after killing him as a fitting memorial? And how in the world did he manage to get him here, all arranged like this, as quickly as he did? Did he perhaps even lure him to this spot to be killed here?"

"Nightmare must really be trying to make an impression on you..." Eugene said, giving me a wary look. "Going to such extravagant lengths as he is."

I didn't like that thought.

"There must be something we are missing," I said, running my hand over my face, staring intently. "I must say...the victim is an enormous man. I think you may be right that he was military."

"Which begs the question...how in the world did Nightmare manage to take someone like this down?" Eugene asked.

"And with so little evidence left behind?" I asked.

This was not boding well for me. I often felt unqualified for these cases, but this one was already beginning to feel as if I was *far* outside my skill level.

"That doesn't matter right now," I said, shaking my head. "There are many questions that are not important right now. They won't help us solve this case." This *game,*

I corrected myself. "What of the scene? What is Nightmare trying to get me to see?" I asked.

"Well..." Eugene said, taking a step back to regard the scene more fully. "The victim is lying at the foot of a grave. Could this be an echo of the other case you once solved in a cemetery? With that young woman? What was her name..." he asked, snapping his fingers, the words eluding him.

"Mrs. Swan," I said, but shook my head. "I don't know. Yes, Felix and I brought flowers to that cemetery, but these ones here are already dead...which I assume means something."

"Him and the flowers..." Eugene said.

"Maybe something to do with the passage of time?" Ronald asked.

I turned to look at him and found him nervously eyeing me. "That's not a bad observation," I said. "And maybe we need to look at this man a bit more closely in order to determine how he died."

I took a step forward again, looking the corpse over. Nothing immediately stood out, except the sheer number of pockets on the front of his coat.

A small triangle of ivory stuck out of the top of the uppermost pocket...right over his heart.

I swallowed, my mouth suddenly dry. I reached out, my heart pounding –

"What are you doing?" Eugene asked.

"Seeing what this is," I said, gingerly closing my thumb and forefinger over the tiny point. I gave it a tug, and stopped...waiting.

Nothing happened.

I pulled it out a little more, and still nothing

happened. I didn't quite know what I had expected to happen, but it had been nothing good.

"It's a letter," Eugene said. "It must be."

He was right, for I had procured a folded piece of paper. One edge had been torn, and the sloppy fold told me that it had been done hastily.

I stared at it for a moment, knowing without a doubt that this note had been written by Nightmare for me, and was not something that had belonged to the gentleman lying here before me.

My heart pounded, as I unfolded it.

The letter within was longer than I had expected, but tightly written. "The handwriting is horrendous..." I said, squinting to try and read the first few words. "It must have been written quickly." That gave me a degree of hope, knowing that Nightmare could have struggled in some way to prepare any of this for me. That meant he was human, which meant he could be defeated.

"What does it say?" Ronald asked, his voice shaking slightly.

I drew in a sharp breath, and began to read.

"*Congratulations. I should like to introduce you to Sergeant McCoy, former soldier turned mercenary...but he is already dead.*"

"Former soldier?" Eugene asked. "That's troubling."

"And mercenary?" I said, my breath catching. "I have only heard tale of men like this." I thought back to what Richard had described about the underbelly of the city, and all the troubles that lurked in the shadows there. "It's certainly unsettling."

"Indeed," Eugene said. "Especially knowing that he used to fight for his country and has since gone rogue."

"Is that all the letter says?" Ronald asked.

"No," I said. I continued to read. "*This is a man who took as many lives as he protected, so it seems fitting that he has finally faced the death so many have met, due to his deeds. Can you truly pity one such as him? Is it not good that he is swept from the face of the earth? Perhaps I have done us all a service.*"

"Sounds like Nightmare fancies himself a bit of a hero," Eugene said darkly.

I nodded. "*He had no family, no friends to mourn his death. He lived alone, worked alone, and died alone. At forty-two years old, he lived a dangerous and unpredictable life. The only consistency in his habits was the Knotted Plank Inn here in London, where he met his end this evening, drinking the same ale he drank every night, not realizing until too late that it was laced with poison. He died right after seeing the face of his killer.*"

"Well, that answers some of our questions," Eugene said, frowning.

"Poisoning..." I said, looking down at the dead man. "That would explain why there are no obvious markings of any kind."

"And we have a name," Eugene said. "McCoy."

"But I don't know how much that is going to help us," I said. "We are already being told he had no friends and no family. There would be no one to question...except for the people at this Knotted Plank Inn."

"Which I guess should be the place we head next," Eugene said. "Right?"

"Hold on a moment, there's still more in this note," I said. "In smaller writing. '*I should warn you not to waste too much time paying your respects to our friend the Sergeant, as you only have until midnight tomorrow to find me. If you aren't able to do so, then I will regretfully have to take another life."*

Icy, biting fear swept over me, encasing my heart. I looked up at Eugene, who stared at me in apparent disbelief.

Take another life?

"Midnight tomorrow?" I breathed. "That means I have a time limit?"

"That's just over twenty-four hours from now," Ronald said, quickly doing the math on the ends of his fingers. "It's not very long."

"No, it isn't," I said, crumpling the letter in my hand, suddenly fuming. "I have only solved a crime that quickly one other time, but I had a great deal of help in doing so."

"We should do our best not to panic right now," Eugene said, stepping over Sergeant McCoy's body to me. "If we have such a limited time, we need to utilize it the best we can."

My head swam, my thoughts chasing one another around the inside of my mind like a pack of dogs after a terrified rabbit.

"You're right." I fought the words out, but when I looked up into Eugene's face, his cerulean eyes grounded me. "Of course. I cannot afford to panic."

"I understand this is all overwhelming right now," he said. "But you will be able to do this, and I will be here to help you. You are not working alone, I promise."

I nodded, feeling cold sweat form a sheen on my forehead.

I looked at the crumpled note in my hand, and opened it again, smoothing it out as best I could. "It is concerning that he is giving me so much information," I said. "Some of what he told me I might not have found for days, if not longer."

"Well, if he gave you a ridiculous timeframe, the least he could do is give you some information to help you along," Eugene said.

"Yes...but why is he giving me so much?" I asked. "That makes me wonder if this is going to be possible to solve."

"Lillian, do not think about a murder that hasn't even occurred yet," Eugene said. "I can see it in your eyes. You are worrying about how and when he is going to strike next, when it may be nothing more than a waste of your time and energy. What we need to focus on is this murder, finding out what we can about Nightmare because of it. That needs to be where we concentrate right now."

"He's right, Miss," Ronald said, coming to my side. "This man's death seems more like a distraction to me than vital information. The game, so to speak, is to find the identity of this Nightmare, yes? Then I think we need to think about him primarily, and how this dead merce-nary could play into learning the truth."

I looked at Ronald and saw determination in his eyes. Fear had been clear before, written in every wrinkle of his face. Now, though, he seemed to have resigned himself to the reality stretched out before us.

"You are right, Ronald," I said. "Our concentration does need to be on Nightmare...who, might I say, has already proven himself to be human." I waved the letter in my hand. "If we can trip him up at all, then maybe we can solve this before it gets any worse."

"Good plan," Eugene said.

"What do we do with this poor fellow?" Ronald asked, nodding his chin toward the sergeant.

"Leave him for now, I guess," I said. "We should go to the police, but every second counts if we are to prevent another murder. And so, I think first we need to head to this inn and see what anyone there knows. Maybe someone saw Nightmare skulking around."

I could see doubt in Eugene's eyes, but he nodded all the same. "Let's get going, then," he said.

He started off up the path, and Ronald and I followed.

I understood Eugene's doubt. If Nightmare had somehow managed to poison the sergeant, watch him die in some lonely alley, and drag the body all the way back out here without anyone noticing...then it was unlikely anyone at the inn had seen him.

Still, I could only hope he had managed to slip up just enough for me to gain an advantage without him knowing.

The cold sweat returned, and I tried to ignore it as it coated my palms. Every minute we took to figure this out, the closer another death loomed over me. I quickened my pace, matching Eugene's stride. He must have been thinking the same thing I was. Time was short.

We reached the car only a few moments later.

"This Knotted Planks Inn," I said, looking at Ronald who made his way around the car to open the door. "Do you know where it is?"

"Well, before tonight I certainly wouldn't have," he said, but then turned and pointed down the street to an intersection washed in the light of the streetlamps standing on the four corners. "We passed by it on our way here, however. I noticed the strange name."

My spirits lifted ever so slightly. "Well, at least things are going our way for now."

"We have plenty of time yet," Eugene said.

"I just hope that someone at the inn can give us information," I said. "Otherwise..."

"Let's not think on that now," Eugene said. "We shouldn't sabotage ourselves before we even begin."

"I know..." I said, but doubts pressed in on me and I found it hard to ignore them.

4

———

I might have thought the name of the Knotted Planks Inn to be clever, if I had not found myself in the situation I did. It might have given me feelings of character, of charm, and perhaps of something wise and old. I might have thought it sounded inviting, pleasant, the sort of place I would wish to visit...

We approached the inn, warm, golden light pouring out of the windows. I could not be sure whether the fogginess in the windows was due to the frigid air outside and what I assumed to be warm insides, or if it was nothing more than a layer of grime so thick that one could not see inside.

Eugene pulled the door open, and I suppressed a shiver. The interior seemed vastly different than the outside had foretold. The floorboards were knotted, all right; knotted and rotting, some of them missing entirely, and they creaked as we stepped inside.

I squinted as my eyes adjusted to the dim light, which came from a few lamps scattered around the room, some on tables, others sitting on the sills of the windows.

There was something almost medieval about the feel of the place.

Ash remained untouched in a hearth made of large, round stones along the southern wall, heaped in the corners, spread far enough apart that a few logs would fit against the sooty back.

Mismatched tables of every shape and size, some of which were badly damaged, were scattered around the room in no particular order. It surprised me how, despite the late hour, almost every bench, stool, and chair was filled...yet there was hardly a voice to be heard.

A few heads swiveled in our direction, one of them belonging to a bald man with a gold ring between his nostrils.

Eugene and I stayed close together as we started around the outside of the room toward the back wall lined with wooden crates of wine. Ronald kept close as well, whistling through his teeth.

We stuck out like black swans amongst pearly white geese. The men gathered here, for they were all men, as far as I could tell, were of the sort that had I never begun investigating murders, I likely never would have laid eyes upon. We lived in entirely different worlds...and unfortunately now I was well out of mine.

I ignored the many passing glances we received – *I* received – and tried to pay attention to my task at hand. It struck me, as we made slow progress between the door and the long bar along the far wall, that perhaps Nightmare had intended to put me in such a precarious situation. Was it to test me? Was it in the hope that one of these criminals, for I had little doubt that was who I found myself in the presence of, would do the job for him and kill me? It seemed possible, but regardless of what his reasoning was, I had only one task now. Or two, really. The first, to make it out alive. The second, to find the identity of Nightmare before the night was through.

We made it through the most densely packed part of the room without incident. Silence fell whenever we passed by, and I waited with baited breath for one of the patrons to jump up and tell us to leave. I began to feel guilty that I had brought Eugene and Ronald with me into this place. Not that I had any more reason to be here myself, but it seemed more appropriate for me than it was for them; I had been in danger more than the pair of them together.

"You look lost," came a voice from the bar.

I cast my eyes toward the cases of wine, but found no one standing there. Prickles washed up my arms, and I turned to see a man sitting alone at the bar.

He had not looked at us, staring vacantly toward the cross-hatched back wall filled with dusty, sealed bottles. He clutched a glass tankard, filled to the brim with golden ale.

I swallowed hard as Eugene situated himself in front of me. "We certainly are not here for the pleasure of it," he said.

"Well, then you would be alone in that," the man said, taking a long draw from the tankard.

I turned to look over my shoulder, and eyed the relatively silent guests, most of whom seemed more interested in the food or drinks before them than the companions beside them.

"You'd better find what you came for," the man said. "Before you overstay your welcome."

I stepped out from behind Eugene. "We are looking for information about Sergeant McCoy," I said.

A few people at the nearest table turned at the sound of my voice, or the mention of the name, I couldn't be sure.

"Are you, now?" the man asked. He turned his gaze to me finally. "You missed him," he said, hoisting his tankard to his lips once again. "He was here about an hour ago."

My face flushed, and I gave Eugene a quick glance.

Our new friend must have noticed, because he turned back to me, his brows arching. "What do you need?" he asked. "With McCoy's particular...skills, I am sure there would be someone else here to fit your needs."

I didn't know if we could trust this person. In fact, I was almost certain there would not be a soul in this place we *could* trust, and that was going to make this all the more difficult.

"Might I ask who we are speaking with?" Eugene asked, apparently thinking along the same lines I was.

"They call me Flint," he said. "And no, I do not have what you are looking for."

"Which is what?" I asked. "How can you be so sure that you know what it is we need?"

Flint smacked his lips, eyeing his nearly empty tankard with regret. "I have been in this business long enough to know you are desperate for someone to fix your problems, desperate enough to come down here to look for help. That's your business." He glanced over at the wall, jutting his chin in that direction. "There's a job

board over there. Take a look and see what you can find.
And if you need to, leave your contact information and
someone will be in touch."

I turned to look in the direction he'd indicated, and
found there was indeed a board with notes pinned to it. I
swallowed hard and opened my mouth to speak, but
Eugene spoke first.

"We aren't here for a hit job," he said. "We need information about this Sergeant McCoy."

Flint's tankard hit the bar top with some force,
sending tremors down its length. I jumped at the harsh
sound, and a few heads at the nearby table turned.

"I already told you, he – "

"What's this about?"

The door behind the bar had swung open, and a
stunningly beautiful woman strode out. Shapely, yet a bit
older than I first suspected, she glared at Flint with
intense green eyes.

At once, Flint ducked his head, as if to hide behind
his empty tankard. "Sorry, Rose."

"What's got you all worked up?" she asked, taking his
tankard as naturally as if she did this in her sleep. She
turned those intense eyes upon us, as sharp as a dagger.
"Who are these people?"

"Good evening, Miss," Eugene said, stepping up to the
bar. "We are here looking for – "

She cocked her hip and chuckled. "Darling, I'm
guessing you're lost," she said, not unkindly. "You must be
looking for the Jilted Orchid Inn, just a few streets to the
north. You can't miss it, really."

I stepped out from behind him, and her eyes passed
over to me immediately. "This is no mistake," I said. "We

are here looking for information about Sergeant McCoy."

The woman's brows rose and she blinked a few times. "Well, it isn't often we receive intentional newcomers," she said, sliding Flint's tankard under the tap. She gave it a comfortable pull, and without looking, began to fill it. "You do realize what this place is, yes?"

"We do," I said. "And it is very important that you tell me what information you can."

Rose pursed her lips, looking thoughtful. "Well, Sergeant McCoy is a quiet fellow. You just missed him. Couldn't have left three quarters of an hour ago."

"So we've heard," I said. They must not have realized that anything had happened to him. Would it be my responsibility to tell them? I couldn't see why, unless it would aid my purpose. "What I want to know is about him. I need to know anything you can tell me."

"There truly isn't much to tell," she said with a shrug. "All I know is that he lives alone here in the city. Apparently he was raised in Yorkshire, but hasn't lived there in almost thirty years. Never married, never had any children." She shook her head. "He leads a dangerous life."

"Yes, we know about him being a mercenary," Eugene said. I noticed he chose his words carefully, so as not to allude to the man in the past tense. "Has he ever mentioned any sort of enemies?"

Rose laughed as she slid the tankard down the bar back to Flint.

Eugene grimaced. "Yes, I realize he must have had a great many enemies. But were there any in particular that he mentioned? Ones that might have repeatedly given him a problem?"

Rose wiped her eye, still chuckling. "Oh, that's quite humorous," she said. "Oh...but no, I can't think of one in particular. You have to understand, asking whether or not these people have enemies is like asking if they have to eat to survive. It's inevitable."

Her eyes narrowed as she regarded the three of us.

"Why are you really here?" she asked. "You know McCoy by name, which means you have some connection to him. People don't just waltz in here without reason."

"My reasons are my own," I said, matching the intensity of her stare. "It matters not to you."

She folded her arms. "I should say that it does," she said. "This is my inn, and I have – "

The door at the back of the inn burst open, and a man with a dirty, sooty face came rushing inside. "It's McCoy!" he shouted, pointing back out into the darkness behind him. "He's dead! In the cemetery!"

"He what?" Rose asked, abandoning the tankard of ale she had been filling.

Flint turned to regard the man at the door while others leapt to their feet. Many hurried out the door after the man, as he disappeared again into the night.

I looked at Eugene as the room descended quickly into chaos.

"We should go..." Eugene said under his breath.

I didn't need to be told twice.

Rose, eyes shooting in our direction, said nothing as we made our way back toward the door. I could feel her gaze on the back of my head as we exited the inn.

Shouts and carrying on drifted from the cemetery behind the inn, and I had to force myself not to glance in that direction. I had already seen what I needed to there.

As Ronald helped me into the car, his eyes sweeping up and down the street for any possible interference, I began to wonder if Nightmare had not been in that room somewhere, watching me, listening to me. I couldn't imagine he would have gotten far after killing McCoy like he had...

Ronald closed the car door and made his way to the front, sliding inside.

As he closed the door, silence fell over us all. My ears rang, even as the worried shouts of the patrons at the inn could still be faintly heard.

"Where to now, Miss Crawford?" Ronald asked.

I blinked, my eyes burning. Between the late hour and the biting wind, I was drained of most of my energy. "I...don't know," I said. "I need a moment to think."

"I'm afraid to say it, but I think that Rose believes we were somehow involved with Sergeant McCoy's death," Eugene said in a low murmur.

"She wouldn't be wrong," I said. "If it weren't for this game of Nightmare's, then McCoy would likely still be alive in there now."

I glanced out the window at the inn, the lights in the windows still burning bright.

"We learned nothing about him," I said. "Nothing that Nightmare didn't already tell us. If anything, that felt like a waste of time."

"Then perhaps, Miss, might I make a suggestion?" Ronald asked, gazing at me in the reflection of the rearview mirror.

"I am certainly open to them," I said heavily.

"Didn't the initial letter you received say that you could go to the police for help?" he asked. "I wonder if it would be wise to involve them before any other deaths occur."

"I agree," Eugene said. "With a man like McCoy, who used to be in the military, it might be enough to interest them."

"We have no other leads, I suppose," I said, pinching the bridge of my nose, my head beginning to throb at the temples. "Maybe they could show us where to head next."

As Ronald drove us toward the metropolitan police station, the main headquarters in London, I began to think.

"Something is not sitting right with me..." I said, looking at Eugene.

"What is that?" he asked.

"Typically, with these sorts of investigations, I have one death to look into, and I can find enough evidence to point me to one particular person. How can I even be sure that Nightmare had any association with this Sergeant McCoy?"

"Well, he certainly seemed to know a great deal about him," Eugene said. "That seems likely grounds for some understanding of the man, some tie to him."

"Maybe," I said. "It's just...something doesn't seem to fit. It feels like I am chasing smoke."

"It is quite the daunting task, I will give you that," Eugene said. "But we are still early on. We have only gone to one place to investigate thus far."

"Yes, and it was a place that Nightmare pointed out to me specifically," I said. I frowned, shaking my head. "I just feel as if I must have missed something there, something he must have meant for me to notice."

"Maybe it will come to you later," Eugene said. "Let's see what the police have to say. If we need to, we can always go back."

"That's if that Rose would even let me in the door," I said. "As you said, she might think we were somehow involved in the death. And if she has a room full of criminals at her beck and call..."

Eugene's face fell as he realized what I was saying.

We reached the police station in short order; at this hour, there were hardly any other cars on the streets to speak of. Eugene and I tromped into the main headquarters at half past one in the morning, Ronald choosing to remain with the car, the deepest and coldest parts of the night clinging closely to us.

It surprised me to see the number of people packed into the main room. Lines a dozen long stretched from counters along the far wall; women moaned in agony, men shouted. If it weren't for men standing about in police uniforms, I might have thought we were at the wrong place.

I hurried over to the nearest officer who did not appear terribly busy. "Pardon me, sir," I said. "I am here to report a crime – "

"Get in line," he said without any emotion. "You'll be seen as soon as someone is able."

I blinked at him. Perhaps he did not believe me, or had misheard. "I'm sorry, did you not hear me?" I asked. "I have information about a murder that I should like to – "

"You will have the chance to say your piece when you

reach the front of the line," the officer said, his gaze hardening as it fell on me. "I cannot help you."

"You cannot? Or you will not?" I asked, eyes narrowing.

He met my gaze with a blank stare of his own. "I'm sorry, Miss. Everyone here has a story to tell, each as bad as the last. Now if you get in line, you will have the chance to tell yours."

"Someone has just died, and there is another person in danger," I said, my voice rising. "Don't you understand?"

"Easy, now, my dear..." Eugene said, sweeping me away from the officer.

My hands shook as he led me to stand in the nearest line beside him.

"I understand you're frustrated," Eugene said. "But we must be patient."

"We don't have *time* to be patient," I said, glancing up at the round clock on the wall above the door, its ornate hands moving at frightening speed. Was that truly how quickly seconds passed? How was it already almost two in the morning? "Why is he not taking this seriously?"

"I don't believe he isn't taking it seriously," he said. "He is just doing his job."

"I would have thought he would take us right to the front of the line," I said, scowling. "Wouldn't a murder be enough of a reason to do so?"

"Unless half the people here are crying wolf," Eugene said. "Everyone here is desperate, looking for help. We cannot fault them for that. And many of them are likely experiencing true emergencies, as well."

I looked around the room, and saw the desperation in

their faces. He wasn't wrong. Frightened mothers, worried fathers...people looking for friends, needing help, at their wit's ends. There would be no other need to be here, it had to be serious.

I drew in a deep breath, trying to calm my frantic nerves. "You're right," I said. "Of course." The world continued to go on around me, even if it felt as if everything was beginning to cave in on me and my own personal sphere.

I needed to control my emotions, not allow them to run rampant.

It was arduous, but soon we reached the front of the line. It couldn't have been more than a quarter of an hour, but with the crowding and the low and frightened murmurs of those around us, I began to feel like a bird picked clean of its feathers; exposed and raw.

"Next," came the thoroughly uninterested voice at the counter. A bespectacled man looked up at me with heavy eyelids and a grim expression. I imagined hearing horrendous stories day after day would leave one feeling rather jaded. "What is your trouble?"

"I am here to report a murder," I said, drawing Nightmare's letter from my satchel. "I have information in this letter about it."

The spectacled man's eyes narrowed behind his lenses, and he pushed them up the bridge of his nose before taking the letter in my outstretched hand. He gave it a quick read through before turning to one of the officers standing at the door behind him, and gave him a nod. "Officer Willowby will hear your story," he said. "We will do what we can to help."

It hardly put me at ease as he immediately cried,

"Next!" before we had even skirted around the table toward the door behind him.

Officer Willowby could not have been any older than Eugene and I. Bits of his corn blonde hair peeked out underneath his black hat like stalks of wheat. "Right through here," he said, standing aside to let Eugene and I pass. He showed us into a small, windowless room with a battered table in the middle and two chairs to each side. "Please, sit where you like," he said.

Eugene pulled the chair out nearest to him, and offered it to me. I sat, and he took the chair beside mine.

Officer Willowby sank down into the seat opposite us and scooted his chair closer to the table. "There we are," he said, folding his hands in front of himself. "Now...what can we do for you?"

"We are here to report a murder," I said. "A man by the name of Sergeant McCoy is lying dead in the St. Peter's Cemetery here in London."

Officer Willowby's eyes narrowed slightly. "A murder, you say?" he asked. He snapped his fingers, and an officer appeared as if out of nowhere. Like a chameleon, he had blended in to the wall he had been standing against. The two policemen muttered in low tones together for a moment and I detected the words, "Send...out to...investigate."

The second officer nodded and disappeared through the back door.

"How did you discover this murder?" Officer Willowby asked, procuring a slender piece of paper and a pen and pressing the writing end to the page.

I set the letter from Nightmare on the table, pushing it toward him. "In this letter," I said.

Officer Willowby eyed the letter with mild curiosity. He picked it up and gave it a quick read, his eyes sweeping with deft practice over the words. He glanced at me over the top of the page. "And you say there was indeed a body at this St. Peter's Cemetery?" he asked.

"Yes," I said with a nod.

"The letter says nothing about a body," Officer Willowby said, turning the letter around so that I could see it.

I frowned. "Yes it does – " But then I stopped, turning a wide-eyed gaze to Eugene. "It doesn't."

Eugene retrieved the letter, reading it through once again. "The only thing he says here is that he is a serial killer."

"Yes, and we receive these sorts of letters all the time," Officer Willowby said with a dismissive wave of his hand. "These wild pranks pop up regularly, believe it or not."

"But how?" I asked. "I went to the cemetery, and found a dead body, just like the letter said."

"The letter never specified *what* you might find," Officer Willowby said. "Now, this doesn't mean I doubt that you found a body. Your presence here clearly shows that you must be telling the truth."

"Of *course* I'm telling the truth!" I said.

"But there may be no connection to your letter. I must tell you that it is not terribly uncommon for criminals to dump their victims in cemeteries. We've found several such abandoned corpses in cemeteries over the past year."

I could only sit there and stare at him.

"I understand your skepticism and in no way doubt your expertise on the matter," Eugene said. "But we are quite concerned that this letter is real. Miss Crawford is, as the letter claims, a private detective."

Officer Willowby shrugged. "And?"

I blinked. "And I would imagine this would be something you would be keen to take a bit more seriously," I said, trying not to snap at him.

"We will keep it in mind," he said.

Fuming, I pulled out the other letter that I'd found in Sergeant McCoy's front pocket, and with a flick of my wrist, cast the note onto the table.

The man across from me picked it up, reading it. "I understand your concern, but this is not signed. There is no way to know that these two letters were written by the same individual."

"You *cannot* be serious," I exclaimed. "The proof is all right there, in front of you! It all lines up – "

"Please, Miss Crawford, I can see that your emotions are getting the better of you," Officer Willowby said.

I stood to my feet, slamming my palms flat down onto the table. "Officer, do you not realize that if you do *not* take this seriously, someone else is likely to die at midnight tomorrow?"

Officer Willowby stared up at me, searching my face. "Yes, I do realize that," he said. "And I *am* taking it seriously. What I am trying to tell *you* is that I have seen situations like this before...and they are something you simply cannot put too much stock in. Do you think every threat we have seen like this has come to fruition?"

I hesitated. I could only speak for *these* letters, knowing full well that I understood what I was talking about.

"Not to mention that the sheer number of violent

deaths that occur in this city, both murder and otherwise, can hardly be calculated. It is very simple for someone to claim another death by tomorrow, as there is a high probability there will *be* one."

My jaw clenched. "You are missing the point."

"Oh, no, Miss Crawford, I believe you are missing the point," Officer Willowby said, pocketing his notepad; I'd noticed he'd hardly written a thing upon it. "I have seen many letters, just like this one...even signed with ridiculous names like *Death Walker* or *Vengeance.*" He stopped, and sighed. "What you need is to head home and get some rest. You'll see in the morning that this was all just an unfortunate prank, nothing more."

I glared at him. "And what if it's not?" I asked.

He shrugged. "I don't know what else I can tell you that would convince you," he said. "You truly do not need to worry yourself so much. Allow us to take care of it for you. That is our job, after all."

A job I might feel comfortable leaving to you, if you were taking it more seriously.

"Very well," Eugene said. "We have done our due diligence by coming by and telling you what we know. I suppose we cannot force you to do anything else."

"We are doing all we can with what we know," Officer Willowby said. "I have sent men, as you witnessed, to investigate the body at the cemetery. If you knew the time and place that the next death would be happening, we would of course send officers down there as well. If you learn anything else, please come back and tell us. Until then, this is nothing more than a bluff."

"A bluff..." I said.

"As many others have turned out to be," Officer Willowby said. "Most of them, in fact."

"All right, then," Eugene said. "Thank you for your time."

Officer Willowby nodded. "Have a good evening." And with that, he exited the room out the same door that he had sent the other officer through.

5

___

"Maybe Officer Willowby was right..." I said, my voice breaking the silence.

Eugene looked up from his place in the armchair beside the fireplace in Richard's study. A book lay open on his lap, his legs crossed to prop it up. He looked quite comfortable, which put me somewhat at ease given the night we had been having.

The clock on the mantlepiece chimed, and I listened intently. *Bing. Bing. Bing. Bing.*

A sudden, cold shiver rushed down my spine. Four in the morning. Time was moving far more quickly than I ever remembered it going.

Eugene regarded me in silence, waiting for me to speak. I had almost forgotten that I had spoken.

I hesitated.

"I take it that you are ready to discuss all this now?" Richard asked from the chair across from Eugene. He looked up at me, where I had been leaning against the hearth for the better part of an hour now. I had told him that I had not quite wrapped my mind around everything we had learned and seen, and I needed time to consider it all.

"Yes," I said. "First, I simply cannot seem to kick the idea that this is all real. Between the timing of the letter, the discovery of the body with the letter I *know* was meant for me..." I straightened, my back beginning to ache. "I do not believe in coincidence. There is no such thing."

Eugene closed his book. "Words of wisdom," he said.

"Agreed," Richard said. "I have never experienced a coincidence in my life that turned out to be truly chance. Given the logical way you have considered this, I shall agree with you and say that I, too, believe this Nightmare to really have targeted you and sent those letters."

"...But?" Eugene asked. "There is a caveat. I can hear it in your voice."

"I do wonder if I should just scrap the idea all together, as Officer Willowby said," I said. "I had not considered that there could be other criminals, or pranksters, who write letters much like this one. This Nightmare surely isn't the only person to have used such tactics. I do not know why I didn't consider that in the first place. I allowed my fear to get the better of me."

"You have witnessed the instability of others just in your short time in this profession," Richard said, setting his own book down on the low table beside him. The warm glow from the lamp beside him washed his face in its comforting light, which seemed such a stark contrast to the horrors we were discussing. "What better way to get someone's attention without giving up one's identity than with an anonymous letter?"

"Right," I said, scratching my chin, pursing my lips. "Which makes me wonder if I have not been taken in."

"Yet you have said that you believe these letters are real," Eugene said.

"I do..." I said. "But how do I know this Nightmare is not simply tricking me? How can I be certain he will strike again at midnight?"

Eugene frowned. "I suppose that was Officer Willowby's point, wasn't it?"

I nodded, staring down into the hearth, watching the flames lick the fresh logs that Hughes had brought in for us a short while ago.

"I wonder what will happen if I ignore the letter as he suggested," I said.

"The choice is yours, Lillian," Richard said. "You cannot allow Nightmare to bully you into doing this. If you keep playing his game, then he will keep playing too."

"Yes, but what if he keeps playing even if I choose to stop?" I asked.

"He cannot force you to," Eugene said. "It isn't as if he would waltz in here and make you go out into the streets looking for dead bodies. Besides..." He gave me an understanding look. "You cannot prevent every murder that happens in this city. And if Officer Willowby is to be believed, there are a great many of them."

I sighed, shaking my head. "I know full well that I can't prevent them...but for the first time, I am *aware* that people are dying outside of the cases I take on. It seems that every time I find one criminal, another pops up in his place."

"Another four or five," Richard corrected. "I hate to

say. Eugene is right, though. There would be no way that you would know if Nightmare continued on his spree."

"What if I am the only one who can find him?" I asked.

"That's awfully presumptuous of you," Richard said. "Do not mishear me; I think you are a brilliant detective. But you are not the *only* detective, and certainly not the only detective with experience."

"So, you are suggesting that I just leave this for others to resolve?" I asked. "What about those who could die?"

"Could, I think, is the operative word in this situation," Eugene said. "We don't know that anyone else is going to die. We don't even know if Nightmare killed that Sergeant McCoy. It would have been very easy to say everything he did in the letter, to speak to the patrons at the inn, and take the credit for the kill himself."

I paused, considering. "I had not thought of that," I said. "But this brings me to another thought...which is to wonder if I know Nightmare, or have encountered him before."

The chilling silence that met my words made my stomach twist into knots. Eugene and Richard glanced across the room at one another, Richard shaking his head, Eugene's brow furrowed.

"It is entirely possible," I went on. "And if he is going around killing these people *because* of me, then I have no choice but to step in and stop it."

Richard drew in a long breath, exhaling heavily, clearly reluctant to speak. "I can see your point, and it is something I've considered," he said. "At the very least, if this Nightmare is real, is truly trying to goad you into playing this twisted game, then he has to have heard of you in some capacity. He is at least aware of your accomplishments and the cases you've solved."

"Which leads one to believe it is also possible he knows you even better than that," Eugene said, worry creasing his forehead further. "It could be someone you know or someone you have dealt with before."

"Exactly," I said. "That is why I am not willing to write this off so quickly."

Richard rose to his feet, striding to the fireplace to stand beside me. He gave me a hard look, the wrinkles of concern in deep contrast from the light of the fire, making him seem rather menacing. "You have already thought of someone, haven't you?"

Eugene looked at me with surprise. "Have you?" he repeated. "Who?"

I tried to swallow, but my throat had grown tight. "Immediately, I thought of Mr. Ward."

Richard's eyes brightened with recognition before quickly darkening again with the understanding of precisely what that could mean. He strode away from me, rubbing his forehead.

"Mr. Ward?" Eugene asked, frowning. "I vaguely recognize that name, but I can't quite place it."

"Do you remember the case that I solved in a single night?" I asked. "Felix and I went to the home of a Mrs. Carter, who suspected her husband was being targeted for murder?"

Eugene nodded. "I do now, yes."

"Mr. Lee was killed when the lights went out that night, while Mr. Ward and some of his other associates thought him to be Mr. Carter, who was their enemy. They were embezzling money, and wanted power in the company for themselves."

"Mr. Ward is a powerful man," Richard said from near his desk. "Even in prison, he could likely still have influence over events unfolding out here in the rest of the world."

That made me all the more nervous. "He had no qualms about murdering Mr. Lee," I said. "He did not show any sign of caring whatsoever about it. In fact, he seemed keen to kill Mr. Carter, too, and any of the rest of us who might have gotten into his way."

"A man as well-connected as he is..." Eugene said, running his fingers through his hair. "He could have bought someone off to do this."

"And he made it perfectly clear that he was not going to forget what happened," I said. "He didn't die, even though I took a shot at him."

Eugene's face fell. "I remember how much that troubled you after it happened."

"Perhaps it would have been better if you *had* killed him," Richard said.

I gave him a look, but he shrugged.

"If this somehow *is* him, coming back to haunt you out of revenge, then his death would mean none of this would be happening in the first place," he said.

I frowned. "He certainly was all too happy to cause as much damage as he could if it benefitted him," I said.

"What would coming after you accomplish for someone like him, though?" Eugene asked. "Aside from vengeance? You just said yourself that as long as something benefitted him, he was willing to do it. Would your torment do anything for him apart from give him enjoyment?"

"That is how some people operate, Mr. Osbourn," Richard said, crossing his arms. "To some, the acquisition of power *is* the end goal."

"But then what?" Eugene asked. "It isn't as if driving Lillian out of her wits would help him. It would not spare him the penalty for his crimes."

"Not in any way that I can see..." I said. Goosebumps appeared on my arms. "Still, I do not like to think that I might be the personal target of someone like him."

"It's a place to start," Richard said. "Plausible even, given your history with him."

"Honestly, out of all the culprits I have encountered, I think he is the only one capable of such forethought," I said. I held my hand out, counting on my fingers. "Mr. Morse, Mr. Burton...then there was Mr. Ward, and Eliza... oh, and of course, there was Mr. Dieter." I bristled. "He was terribly unpleasant, and might have been capable of this, if he thought I had ruined his business and reputation as I did Mr. Ward's."

"And my sister," Eugene said, his face falling. "But she is no longer with us, either."

"Right..." I said. I supposed he hadn't realized that I had *intentionally* left her out to spare his feelings.

"Mr. Ward is the most connected, and likely the most influenced by your interference," Richard said. "You stepping in and saving Mr. Carter cost him everything. Yes, your involvement in every case has been of great detriment to all those who found themselves in prison, but I believe he had the most to lose out of all of them."

"My thoughts precisely," I said in a low voice.

It did not give me any peace to have settled on a possible suspect. In fact, it made the whole ordeal all the more terrifying. Now I had a lead...and facing that man again would certainly be something out of a nightmare. He had frightened me more than almost all the others I'd confronted, seeming the most violent and volatile of the lot.

"This will be simple enough to check," Richard said. "All you need to do is discover which prison he is being kept in, and go see what you can find out."

"You mean go and speak with him?" I asked, trying to suppress a shiver.

Richard nodded. "There would be no safer place," he said. "You would be better protected than he."

I glanced at Eugene, and he nodded agreement.

Horrific images flashed through my mind of sitting in a tight, cramped room similar to the one at the police station, with Mr. Ward across from me wearing a terrible grin before lashing out to wrap his thick hands around my neck and throttle me, before anyone had the chance to intervene.

But I couldn't let such a fear get the better of me.

"I should go, then," I said, starting toward the door. "There is no reason to sit around and think on it any longer – "

Eugene took hold of my hand, stopping me in my tracks.

I looked back at him,

"Its half past four in the morning," he said.

I blinked. "And?" I asked.

Richard peered around Eugene, who had blocked my sight of him across the room. "You aren't even going to be able to get into the prison at this hour," he said. "Likely not for some hours, yet."

I looked up at Eugene, who nodded.

"You should try and get some rest," he said.

"How can I?" I asked. "I can't possibly sleep now."

"I understand," Eugene said. "But you should still try."

I frowned at him.

"He's right, you know," Richard said. "You need to save your strength."

I glared at the both of them, but I knew they were right. There was nothing I could do, not at the moment.

"Fine..." I said. "But I am not going to sleep."

6

———

I did sleep, in the end. It was nearing five-thirty after Hughes had brought me a hot bowl of soup and some warm, crusty bread that sleep overtook me right in the chair I had settled myself into. I dozed hard for almost three hours.

I only awoke when bright sunlight pressed against my eyelids, my cheeks burning from its direct, piercing beams. When I tried to open my eyes, I winced and covered my face, the intensity of the light almost painful. Turning my head, peeling my watery, heavy eyes open, I allowed my vision to clear and sharpen.

My neck ached as I felt the velvet of Richard's armchair against my forehead, and realized that I had not moved from the position I'd landed myself in just a few hours before. I rubbed my eyes, trying to clear them of sleep, and went to move my head...when whispers met my ears from nearby.

"...Best if we try to convince her to stay here," said a low voice. It was Richard's; I could tell because of the cadence of his tone. "No telling what might happen if she does leave today."

"You really don't think it's a good idea for us to go and see if this Mr. Ward had anything to do with this?" It was Eugene this time, also keeping his voice low.

I couldn't see them out of my periphery, and so assumed that they must have been standing behind me, near the door.

"I don't," Richard said. "I've been really thinking about this, and what is the harm in her simply ignoring it all? What harm is there to her directly, I mean?"

"She's concerned about those who might die because of her decision," Eugene said. "And to be fair, her concern is not without good reason." It pleased me to hear him standing up for me as he was.

"She still has a choice in the matter, though," Richard said. "As we said last night, he cannot force her into anything."

"What if the letters from him continue to arrive? What if he sends one after another after another? What if someone dies every time he sends a letter?" Eugene asked. "Who knows how persistent this Nightmare could be."

Silence stretched from one heartbeat to the next.

Richard said, "I do not want to lose her, and if you really love her, Eugene, you will see the sense in this. We *must* protect her for her own good."

"I understand your concern, I truly do," Eugene said, and I noticed an edge to his voice as it grew in volume. "But I also realize this is a matter of principle to Lillian. If this man truly is as insane as we think, then she feels it is her duty to stop him. I know her heart, and she feels that if she ignores Nightmare, then she is turning her back on all his future victims."

"And what if this is not where it ends?" Richard asked. "What if he changes the game? What if he does not follow his own rules? What if there *are no rules?*" He scoffed. "You do not seem to understand. There is no guarantee that any of this will end – "

"It will end if she and I find him," Eugene said. "If we can bring him to justice, then all this will be over. It may be the only way that it will."

Icy stillness settled over the room. While my neck throbbed now that the nerves had fully awoken, I resisted the urge to move it a great deal. I didn't think it wise to let them know I was listening in on their conversation...even if it was about me.

"She will wake soon," Richard said. "I can only hope you know you are willingly taking her into danger. I know she is skilled, and she has done an incredible job as a private detective...but she may have met her match with this, and it would be wise to take whatever precautions you can."

"I will do just that," Eugene said.

Footsteps quickly faded, and a moment later, I heard a heavy sigh.

A spasm in the muscle of my neck made me snap my head up into its rightful position, and I massaged the tense spot.

"Good morning," said Eugene warmly, slipping into the chair beside mine.

I blinked, pretending to be groggy. "Morning..." I mumbled, and stifled a genuine yawn. "Ow...who let me fall asleep in this chair?" I asked.

Eugene smiled. "Last I remember, you refused to go up to your room when we asked you...several times."

I frowned, and sighed. "Yes, well, maybe it's best I didn't," I said. "We can be on our way sooner. What time is it?"

"Just before ten."

"Ten?" I exclaimed, leaping to my feet. "Why didn't you wake me sooner?"

"You needed your rest," he said.

"I need to solve this case, is what I need to do." I reached up to check the state of my hair and groaned, rushing to a mirror along the wall. I combed my fingers through the tangled, dark ends, grimacing at my reflection. It didn't matter that dark circles had appeared beneath my eyes, or that the whites of my eyes were streaked with red. "We don't have time to waste."

Eugene did not argue further with me, but instead obeyed as I ordered him around. "Fetch my satchel! Throw me that pair of gloves! No, not that hat, the *other* one!"

I barely had time to say goodbye to Richard before trying to rush out the door. Hughes met us there, with a small parcel of food tied up in a checkered napkin. "You'll need your strength," the butler told me, and I noticed before hurrying to the car that there was a flicker of worry in his gaze. I ignored it, as Ronald opened the door and helped me inside.

We were halfway to the nearest police station to Mr. Carter's house, which Eugene had suggested might be where they would have record of where Mr. Ward had been sent, when the warm, comforting scent of breakfast became too much to resist.

I cared little for propriety as I snatched chunks of roasted meat and potatoes from inside the parcel, marveling at how hungry I was and how good it all tasted. I licked the buttery bits of the potato still sticking to my fingers, glancing at Eugene. "It's difficult to believe it has not yet been twenty-four hours since we all were sitting together for dinner last night, talking about Marie's wedding, enjoying ourselves..." I said, reaching for another slice of the roasted meat. "I cannot believe how hungry I am."

"Well, you haven't exactly been sitting on your hands idle," he said. "If anything, all the running we have been doing, all the searching and lack of sleep, was bound to catch up with you."

"Aren't you hungry?" I asked, pushing the small parcel toward him.

He shook his head. "I ate with Richard this morning, just before you woke. You need it. You go ahead."

I didn't exactly mind, or push, and so by the time we reached the police station, I had polished off the whole meal. I made a mental note to thank Hughes profusely for that upon returning home. If he had decided he wanted to take care of me like that, he would be welcome to do so at any time.

It didn't take us long to find Mr. Ward's whereabouts. Eugene had been right; the station did indeed have a record of his arrest, and where he was taken to serve his time in prison. It seemed that Mr. Turner had been mentioned on the report, which the officer read off to us in a half-hearted malaise, but I had no need to inquire about him. He might have been the one to kill Mr. Lee, but Mr. Ward was the mastermind behind the whole fiasco.

Ronald knew precisely where the prison was, and the flicker of fear in his gaze at the mention of its name set my own nerves alight.

"You seem to be worried about going here," I asked him as we started away from the police station. "Is there something we should know before we go?"

Ronald shifted in his seat, eyes fixed straight ahead. His hands gripped the steering wheel more tightly. "I...know someone who was sent here," he said. "A cousin of mine."

"I'm sorry to hear that," I said. I fought the urge to ask more questions; it was clear the whole idea made him uncomfortable.

"It happened a long time ago," Ronald said with a nervous laugh. "It's...it's no trouble, really. Not anymore."

Eugene gave me a worried look, and I once again had to fight the urge to ask a question about it. *That isn't important right now.*

"What, uh...what should we know about this place?" Eugene asked, cautiously.

"It's dark," Ronald said, shaking his head. "Very dark. And cold." He paused for a moment. "That's all I remember, really."

"You've been there?" I asked.

He nodded, still not turning around, keeping his eyes fixed squarely on the road in front of him. "I have. But as I said...it was many years ago."

He rolled his shoulders. "It's where they keep the worst of the worst," he said. "It's quite terrible, really."

I couldn't take it anymore.

"What happened to your cousin?" I asked. "What did he do?"

"Oh..." Ronald said in a falsely surprised voice. "He... well, he tried to steal some jewels belonging to a distant member of the royal family."

I stared at the back of his head.

"How did he manage that?" Eugene asked.

"He didn't," Ronald said. "He tried, as I said. They caught him just before he could escape."

"I didn't realize there was a thief in your family," I said.

"Neither did the rest of us, until he was caught," Ronald said with a tight, brief smile in the rearview mirror. "He was my best friend, too...shows how little I knew him, doesn't it?"

I didn't even know what to say. "I am sorry, Ronald," I said.

"As am I," Eugene said.

We rode in silence for the remainder of the trip. When we reached the prison, I hardly dared speak and break it.

I could see from first sight of the prison why Ronald dreaded it as much as he did. We had crested a hill far outside the city of London itself, and found a low valley tucked between two hills where a solitary, stone structure stood. At first glance, it might have been a castle or something equally old, but as we drew nearer, I noticed the lack of windows, the tall, unscalable towers, and an absurd number of guards posted at intervals. A long, high wall had been erected around it, out of the same stone as the prison itself, and tall, jagged rocks had been set into the top, like a long row of teeth surrounding the whole property.

A small gatehouse stood outside the enormous, steel gates; those must have been installed more recently.

"Are they even going to let us in?" I asked, peering out through the windscreen at the foreboding building seemingly growing right before our very eyes.

"I suppose we will see," Ronald said. "We will just explain who you are, and what you are doing."

I pursed my lips, sitting back against the seat.

"If we look as if we are supposed to be here, then they likely won't give us any trouble," Eugene said as Ronald slowed the car, pulling it up to the gatehouse.

Rain began to pitter-pat against the roof of the car, dotting the windows with tiny, clear orbs that slipped and streaked down the glass.

"Good afternoon," the officer at the gate said. My heart skipped. It really was afternoon already? "How can I help you?"

"Ah, yes, hello," Ronald said. "I bring a Mr. Osbourn and Miss Crawford to visit one of the inmates."

The gatekeeper, a man much older than I would have thought reasonable to be manning the gate, slowly swung his head in the direction of the backseat. His expression remained blank, his wrinkles not revealing skepticism or anger as he stared at me, and then Eugene. "Do you have an appointment?"

The question was directed at Eugene, who sat up a bit straighter. "No," he said. "But we are here on official business."

"We do not allow spontaneous visits," came the

response. "If you must speak with someone, then you are required to make an appointment."

My cheeks burned. "Well, then might we make one now?" I asked. "With you?"

He shook his head. "No," he said. "You'll need to telephone ahead or send a letter in advance, which will be seen by those in charge of these matters, and they will get back to you with a time when you can return."

My anger began to simmer, low at first. "I am sorry, we did not know," I said. "But we have come all this way, and it is of vital importance that we get in to – "

"I am sorry, as well," the man said, seemingly with very little feeling. "I am not the one who makes the rules, simply the ones who enforces them."

My hands balled into fists at my side. *I do not have time for this!* "Sir, I should like to speak with whomever it is that oversees you," I said. "I am a private detective, and I must get in to speak with one of the prisoners."

The man's eyes lit up with interest. "A detective, you say?" he asked. "Do you have any proof?"

My cheeks burned more brightly. "No, I do *not*," I said, trying to keep the anger from my voice. It would not help me to get in any sooner.

"She has us," Eugene said. "I am her assistant, and this is her driver. We can vouch for her."

"I am going to need more than that to prove to me – "

"Good sir, a *murder* has taken place, only last night," I said, cutting through his words with my own. "And *I* am investigating it. I have reason to believe one of the inmates here has some knowledge concerning the crime, and I must speak with him."

The gatekeeper stared at me, his expression

becoming entirely blank again. He did not seem bothered by my anger, not in the least.

"And if I do not speak with the prisoner, then I have reason to believe another murder is going to be taking place. If I am to prevent it, then I must see him," I said.

The gatekeeper still stared at me, and for a wild moment, I thought he had not heard a word I said.

"We understand this is not the proper protocol," Eugene said. "And we appreciate your diligence in ensuring both our safety and your own. It would, however, be a great favor if you could make an exception for us."

I gave Eugene a sidelong glance, grateful he was with me. He could always see to the heart of an issue, past the frustration of the moment.

"We are who we say we are," Eugene went on. "Did you hear of the Culpepper murder? That is a case Miss Crawford solved."

It was clever, picking a case with perhaps the most prominent name.

"I did hear of that one..." the gatekeeper said.

Eugene nodded. "And you might have read in the papers about that young woman who was recently found dead in the cemetery at her husband's grave?"

"Swan or something, wasn't it?" the gatekeeper said.

Eugene nodded again. "That was her, as well."

"My brother was wrongly accused of being the murderer, in that case," I said. "But I discovered it was actually the victim's former employer, whom she had refused to marry. He killed her husband out of jealousy, and then killed her some time later when she refused him again."

Finally, it seemed we had gotten through to the guard. "Let me see what I can do," he said, and wandered back to the gatehouse.

My spirits lifted as I sank back against the seat, sighing with relief. "I suppose we have more proof than I thought we did," I said. "I don't know why I didn't think to mention the cases."

"I imagine much of the city knows of your exploits," Eugene said. "You've said as much yourself, how people have begun to recognize you."

I licked my lips. "You talk as if I am some sort of celebrity."

"Perhaps in a way, you are," he said.

"He's coming back this way," Ronald said.

"You're clear to go in," the gatekeeper said. "You are going to have a guard accompanying you at all times. You are not to see the prisoner alone."

"I wouldn't want to, even if that were a choice," I said, with great conviction.

He signaled to the other guards at the gate, and soon the steel doors swung inward to allow us access.

The ominous stone towers that stood nearby did nothing to fill me with confidence. As we drew closer, they only seemed to grow taller, colder, and more threatening.

We were met at the car as soon as it stopped. Guards flanked us from all sides, all wearing less than friendly expressions.

"I will have to ask you to step out of the vehicle," said a guard to Ronald as soon as he'd opened the door. "It will be returned to you upon your departure."

"You are taking the car?" I asked.

The guard ignored me.

Eugene opened the door beside him, and he likewise was swarmed.

I had barely opened my mouth to protest this treatment when my own door swung outward and a pair of hands tried to grab me. "Excuse me!" I cried, sliding out of their reach.

"Miss, you need to come with us," the guard said, holding his hand out to me as if I were a child.

"I do not need help from the likes of – " I began.

"Lillian, they just want to help you out of the car," came Eugene's voice, speaking over my own to prevent me from saying whatever I might have.

I grimaced, but allowed the guards to help me from the car.

My heart pounded in my chest as they led us, single file, up the stone steps to the menacing, black metal doors. The definitive *clang, clang, clang* of locks being slid home reverberated out to us, and as the doors swung inward with great creaks and groans, I could see why this place troubled Ronald so much.

The front of the prison had not been designed with comfort or hospitality in mind. Instead, the plain stone floors and walls boasted no warmth. The only furnishings were long, wooden benches along the far wall, and a solitary desk in the far corner. Behind it, a man dressed in the same guard's uniform scribbled something down on some paper, another whole stack beside him.

The guards walked us to the man at the desk, who turned to look up at us as we approached. He squinted in the dim light, his hand poised to write again as if frozen in place. "What's with all the pomp and circumstance?" he asked in a nasally voice.

"They have no appointment, but it seems that the gatekeeper spoke to the Captain. They've been allowed through," said the guard at the front of the group.

The man at the desk continued to squint. "The Captain?" he asked. "Well...if he's given permission, then who are we to argue? You may leave them with me."

"Our orders are to remain with them," said the guard.

The man at the desk sighed. "Very *well*. It's as if the Captain thinks someone is going to break *in,* not out these days..." he muttered under his breath, drawing a fresh piece of paper out of the middle of the stack beside him. "Now...who will you be seeing?"

Eugene approached the desk with a wary glance at the guards to either side of him. "A Mr. Ward," he said.

"Mr. Ward...Mr. Ward..." said the man at the desk, rifling through the top ten or so pages at the top of the stack. "W...W....ah, yes, here it is. All right. Oh, that's quite a surprise. You will be his first visitors."

That did surprise me. He had a family, didn't he? Would his wife and children really not have come to see him?

I suppose the shock of what he did was too much for them to bear...

"All right, I will send for him," the man at the desk said. "You may take them to observation room three." He gave Eugene a mirthless smile. "He should join you within the next half hour."

"Half hour?" I protested. "What is going to take so – "

"Thank you," Eugene said.

The guards moved as one as they guided us down a

hall that was almost indistinguishable from the rest of the stone walls around it. I stepped up to Eugene, and spoke in a low voice. "I'm sorry," I said. "I keep speaking out of turn. My mind is just a wreck – "

"It's all right," he said. "Let's just get through this, shall we?"

Once we got to the room that the man at the desk had assigned to us, guards spread out along the wall on both sides of the door, another guard opened it, and the rest of the group filed inside.

The room was not the same as the one I'd been imagining. Instead of a solitary table with chairs on both sides like at the police station, we stepped into a narrow, long room with a window running the length of the long wall opposite us. It took me a minute to realize that it was not a window that looked outside, but into the next room beyond.

Stepping up to the glass, I peered into a room that looked much like the rest of the complex; stone walls and floor, little lighting, and no windows. A metal grate had been fixed into the wall beside the window.

"Mr. Ward will be brought into this room shortly," said one of the guards lining up along the wall behind us.

"Will he be able to see us in here?" I asked.

The guard nodded, adjusting his hat which seemed ever so slightly too big for him. "Yes, but you will be safe, do not worry about that."

I wasn't exactly worried, considering we were surrounded by guards who seemed all too eager to treat us like the prisoners we were not.

"How long will we have?" Eugene asked.

"Ten minutes is all we give his lot," the guard said.

"Oh, sorry. He's kept in sector C, which means that he's one of the most dangerous in the facility. We don't often like to give him more than he deserves."

"Of course," I said. "We appreciate you allowing us to speak with him, all the same."

"I hope you learn what you need," the guard said. "Did I hear rightly that you are a private detective?"

"Yes, I am," I said.

The guard nodded. "You wouldn't be the first to come through here, talking to these monsters. They all seem to know one another, so getting them to rat each other out is a tactic they often use. It works a charm, too."

I glanced at Eugene. "Maybe this won't be a complete waste of a trip after all."

"Hope not," said the guard. "Well, carry on, then." He withdrew back to the wall, growing as still as if he had transformed into a statue of some sort.

Eugene joined me at the glass, peering into the empty room. "This seems like a good idea, the more I consider it," he said. "I am just glad we found him."

"Not too soon, either," I said, shaking my head. I rubbed my arms, a chill setting into my bones. The stone walls encroaching on us from all sides were not helping matters.

We didn't have to wait long, mercifully. The door at the back of the room on the other side of the window soon swung open, and a pair of guards strode into the room...with Mr. Ward between them.

He wore that nasty grin I had seen in my dreams far too many times. He'd lost weight since I had confronted him in the study of the Carter's rowhouse, especially in his once thick neck. How long had it been since I had seen him? Some months, from what I could recall. His large, hulking form seemed less threatening now, but that could be because I was staring at him through a thick pane of glass with guards all around.

His dark, hollow eyes swept the room, and fell upon the glass...upon *me*.

The cold in my bones reached deeper, stronger, as his shadowed eyes pierced into my own. I knew at once that he recognized me; I could see the glint in his gaze. Fear shot through my veins as if I had been shoved into an icy pond, sending shockwaves of shivers down my spine and arms.

It took a great deal of strength not to look away. Instead, I hardened my gaze as I folded my arms across my chest, holding my chin high.

He, in turn, grinned all the wider.

His wrists were fastened in handcuffs behind his back, which I saw briefly as they sat him down in a solitary chair in the middle of the room. They also attached shackles around his ankles to iron rings on the floor. An extra precaution, which I did not mind in the least.

"He recognized you..." Eugene murmured, and I could hear the unease beneath his words.

"Yes, he did," I said. I did my best to smother the fear. "I suppose that is in our favor, isn't it? It will save us time."

The guards moved away from Mr. Ward after he'd been properly secured, lining up against the back of the wall like the guards behind us.

The floor was ours now, which I became keenly aware of as quiet as it was.

I cleared my throat, and looked up at Eugene.

He gave me an encouraging nod. I could see his affection in his gaze, and that he would remain at my side. I knew I would need that support to make it through this ordeal.

"Mr. Ward..." I said, using my best impression of my mother's stern voice. Not that I had to try hard, as I likely used that voice too often in normal conversation with people who did, or perhaps did not, deserve it. "How kind of you to join us."

"Miss Crawford," he said, his grin shining...apart from a sliver of darkness in his bottom jaw. Somehow, in his time here, he'd lost the tooth. "How generous of you to visit me. Tell me, do you make it a habit to gloat at those you put behind bars?"

I had to resist the urge to lash out at him. From what I recalled of him, he had some wit, and would easily find a way to get a rise out of me. I would need to keep a cool head, if I was to get any information out of him.

"Just those I am rather fond of," I said with a fake, telling flash of a grin. "I have come to ask you some questions."

He chuckled, looking away. He appeared as casual as if we had met him at a bistro in the heart of London. "You think just because I am in this position, and you are in yours, that I am going to give away something as valuable as information for free?" He laughed harder, shaking his head. "No. Not a chance."

Eugene shifted beside me, his arms tensing as they brushed against mine.

I wasn't ready to give up yet. Not by a long shot.

"Fine, you wish to make a transaction?" I asked. "I might be willing to oblige."

His eyes narrowed, his grin still wide. "What could you possibly offer me?"

I could think of a few things. "You don't think that I am connected?" I asked. "Do you not suppose my innocent appearance has garnered me the trust of many? Or allowed me to overhear things others would have wished to keep private?"

Mr. Ward did not respond immediately, and I could see the gears of contemplation turning in his mind. His eyes clouded for but a moment before sharpening to a razor's edge. "Information for information," he said. "Fine. I would like to know what you will give me before I answer your questions."

I snorted derisively. "I think not," I said. "Last I noticed, you are the one in prison. I do not think you have any grounds to make that sort of call. You should be grateful I am even willing to negotiate with you."

Mr. Ward's grin did not diminish. "And yet I still have the ability to refuse you, if I so choose."

He was right about that. While I could see that Mr. Ward seemed to be responding well to my demonstrated strength, he might desire to prove his own. I needed to tread a little more carefully, and see this through with cleverness and not bullheadedness.

"Very well," I said. "You have made your point. And I suppose that since I am the one who found you out – "

"And shot at me, no less," Mr. Ward said, a flash in his eyes.

" – That we can come to some sort of agreement. I hardly dare to ask this, but what is something that you would like to know more of?" I asked.

Mr. Ward seemed to like the idea that I was giving the

reins over to him, even just for a moment. He adjusted himself in his seat, his face turned up in thought. "What do I want to know...?" he asked. "What would be of value to me?"

Eugene glanced down at me; I could feel it on the side of my face. I could also sense that he wished to say something to me, to share his thoughts, but didn't dare when Mr. Ward might be able to overhear.

I knew there was no way Mr. Ward could threaten me, and I could always refuse...though he might then refuse to tell me what I wished to know, as well.

It was a gamble, but it was worth it. At least, I hoped it would be.

A glint in his eye told me he'd made up his mind. His grin widened, and I could see so many teeth that it seemed unnatural. "I think I've got it," he said. "Mr. Benjamin Edison...he was recently discovered to have been having an affair with a wealthy woman who later died, yes?"

My skin prickled. Why did he want to know this? He had pointed out a name from a case I had completed so recently. Had that even been in the newspapers?

I couldn't assume he was not getting *any* information from the outside world. He likely had been getting letters from other contacts.

"Don't worry your pretty little head about it..." Mr. Ward said. "All I am looking for is confirmation."

I looked up at him, my face flushing. Was Mr. Edison going to be the target of some sort of blackmail? As far as I knew, Mr. Edison's affair with Mrs. Caroline Yardley had been kept a private matter. It was the sort of information that could damage a man.

Yet Mr. Ward had heard about it, somehow.

My skin grew hot as the anticipation rose. This was certainly not what I had expected, nor something I knew how to handle.

The only thing to do would be to send word to Mr. Edison as soon as I left, warning him of what might be coming his way. All I could hope was that he could ignore it...

I swallowed hard. I needed the information about Sergeant McCoy. Someone else's life could be hanging in the balance.

"Yes," I relented after what seemed like hours, but could have truly only been a matter of moments.

Mr. Ward chuckled. "Good. That's all I needed to know."

I held my tongue, biting back the curses that were flying through my mind. I had taken his bait, and might have kindled a terrible trouble for Mr. Edison. All I could hope was that I could reach him first...and perhaps the guards in the room would be willing to write up a statement for me. I hoped some were paying attention.

"Now...what is it that you wished to know?" Mr. Ward asked.

I knew it might not be wise to come right out and ask him, as he might deflect and dance around it entirely. It was better to start small, and work my way into it.

Though if Nightmare really *was* Mr. Ward, then he would have known that was my true purpose for coming all along.

Perhaps there really is no way for me to win, here...

If Nightmare played by the rules of his own game, then my ultimate goal was to identify him. This would count, wouldn't it? Would I have to definitely tell him, "You're Nightmare!" or some such nonsense?

This could not be over soon enough.

"What do you know of the Knotted Plank Inn?" I asked.

Mr. Ward's smile morphed into a frown of curiosity. "The Knotted Plank, you say? I have never been there myself, but I've worked with plenty of men who have. It's a scummy place, but the sort of place to take care of certain...problems one might have in life." He grinned. "Why?"

"I am on a case right now that has to do with the inn," I said. "And a man who frequents it."

"I see," Mr. Ward said. "And you came to me because of my connections, I assume?"

It amazed me how placidly he spoke for a man chained to the floor. "Yes," I said.

"And what's the name of the man?" he asked.

Again, I did not know whether it would be wise to relent. Not yet, at least. "He is a mercenary," I said. "Ring any bells?"

"A mercenary?" Mr. Ward said. "My dear girl, I associate with men of higher caliber. The men that serve beneath me might dabble with such showy sorts, but I do not trust a mercenary to maintain a sense of decorum. They would entirely ruin whatever job I might need them for."

"Perhaps one of your associates might have – " I said.

"Did you not hear me?" he asked, his face hardening. "I have no need for those sorts. I much prefer to hire an assassin who works undercover. It is far easier to slip poison into someone's drink just before you share a toast with him than it is to have someone corner him in a dark alley with a blunt weapon."

This conversation was quickly deteriorating, and I did not think he was trying to toy with me. He was too proud of his experience for that, of his own importance. He might not have wanted to get his hands dirty, but he had standards about who he would hire to do his deplorable deeds for him.

"So, you came all this way to learn if I knew a mercenary?" he asked. He barked a laugh. "My, what a waste of time this has been for you, hasn't it?"

I said nothing, but chewed the inside of my lip as I tried to come up with something, *anything,* that might help this not feel precisely as he had stated it.

"Is he on the run? Did he kill someone?" he asked.

"He did," I said. He had no need to know that it was not for this case.

"Well, you'll have a time finding him," Mr. Ward said with another chuckle. "Those men can be like ghosts when they want to be. They know how to disappear, to leave no trail."

I frowned, looking up at Eugene.

He licked his lips, glancing through the window at Mr. Ward before returning his eyes to me. "May I ask one question?" he asked me in a low voice.

I nodded, and stepped aside to let him take the window.

"Mr. Ward, we have recently been introduced to someone who calls himself Nightmare. By any chance, is there anything you could tell us about him?"

Mr. Ward let out a barking laugh, throwing his head back, guffawing so hard that one might have thought passing by that he had just been told the greatest joke of all time. When he gathered himself a moment later, he blinked his eyes, tears streaming from them. "Night-mare?" he asked. "Really? That's the best one I've heard since World Eater!" He dissolved into laughter again.

"Mr. Ward, if you would please take this seriously for a moment – " I said.

His laughter cut through my words before he spoke between chuckles. "You've been had, girl," he said. "Who-ever this person is, they are toying with you. They knew you would be easy to fool, and it seems they were right."

My face flushed, and I cleared my throat, looking away as he chortled again.

"I am glad to see your reputation has attracted such... threatening names," Mr. Ward said.

A movement out of the corner of my eye made my heart leap into my throat, and I grabbed for Eugene, only to realize that it was one of the guards pulling himself away from the wall, striding over to Mr. Ward.

"Your time is up, Ward. Back to the pen with you," he said.

"Good luck to you, Miss Crawford," Mr. Ward said over the shoulder of the guard that had bent down to unshackle his ankles. "And thanks for the payment," he added, with a wink.

Icy cold worry plagued my gut as they carted him away, still chuckling even as he disappeared out the far door.

7

"Well...that was terribly unsettling," I said, looking up at Eugene as the guards walked us back out to the enormous, metal front doors of the prison. They had wasted no time in ushering us out of the interrogation room and back whence we came. Hospitality could not be described as one of their qualities.

"I am surprised you were willing to bargain with him as you did," Eugene said. "Though I can hardly blame you for trying..."

The color returned to my face as I laid eyes on Ronald across the courtyard. "I am not at all happy that he brought up Mr. Edison," I said. "Mr. Edison must be notified as soon as we get back to Richard's that he might garner attention from some unpleasant men."

"Will he take kindly to you using his name and reputation as you did?" Eugene asked.

"I can hope that he will see what I did in good faith," I said, though the pit in my stomach told me how little I believed my own words. "I did clear his name of murder, after all."

"Yes, but to make him a target for a man like Mr. Ward – "

"What would you have had me do?" I snapped, rounding on him halfway down the stairs. "Should I have refused?"

Eugene stared down at me, worry creasing his forehead. "I imagine in retrospect, you think you should have," he said.

My eyes narrowed. "That does me no good," I said. "It does no one any good. Who can change the past?"

Eugene sighed, shaking his head. "I do not mean to criticize," he said. "But you must admit Ward is the only one who really walked out of that room with anything of value."

I rolled my eyes, though guilt burned a hole through my stomach. "I realize that," I hissed through my teeth as I stomped down the rest of the stairs. "I did the wrong thing. I made the wrong choice. Is that what you want me to say?"

Eugene took my hand, spinning me toward him. "No," he said. "This whole ordeal is terrible, and I know we have found ourselves in a sticky situation. He asked for information that could ruin Mr. Edison's reputation, and – "

"I know what you are going to say – " I started, the anger bubbling up.

"Listen to me," he said firmly. "Hear me when I say that I know you could see no way out of it. Nor could I. That does not mean, however, that it was the right thing to do."

"What would you have had me do, then?" I asked. "Deny him? And then what?"

Eugene stopped, exhaling heavily. "Lillian, I am not upset with you – "

"Well, you certainly have a strange way of showing that," I said, glaring at him as I approached Ronald. "Let's go."

Ronald blinked at me as I stood next to the door, crossing my arms. How could Eugene say that to me? I would have liked to see how *he* would have handled that conversation.

And yet...I knew he was right, far in the back corners of my mind, the parts where the cobwebs clung and the shadows lurked.

Ronald pulled open the door for me, and I slid inside.

Eugene came around the other side and lowered himself inside. "Allow me to start again," he said. "You handled yourself as best you could, considering the circumstances. I know you had no idea he would ask about Mr. Edison, and you have every intention of warning him in whatever way you can. I'm sure I am not wrong in thinking Ward put you in a precarious situation when we had no idea what he may or may not have known about Nightmare...yes?"

I grumbled for a moment under my breath, and turned to look out the window before Ronald rejoined us in the car. "...Yes," I relented. "Yes, we had no idea."

"Exactly," he said. "And yet, I am sure you agree with me when I say that in retrospect, it would have been better not to answer that question in the first place."

My insides burned, writhing with worry and fury. "Yes, *fine*. Yes! Of course I wish I had not answered his question! I know full well I may have put Mr. Edison in danger, and for what?" I crossed my arms, huffing as Ronald started the engine. "And for what?" I repeated, a little softer.

Eugene sighed. "I don't know," he said.

What did it say that even Eugene could think of nothing uplifting or encouraging to say?

I sank back against the seat, groaning. "This whole ordeal could not have gone any worse."

Eugene shook his head. "Don't say that. It could always have been worse."

I shot him a glare. "I *suppose* he could have broken his chains, smashed the glass, and taken the pair of us out," I snapped. "We learned nothing. *Nothing!*"

Ronald glanced at us in the rearview mirror. "I suppose there is no use in asking about the meeting?"

"No," I said, passing my glare on to him, as well. "I gambled, took a risk, and lost. What more is there to say?"

Ronald shifted his gaze to Eugene. "He wasn't Nightmare then, I take it?"

Eugene shook his head. "Evidently not, unless he is very good at playing ignorant. He seemed to have no idea about the dead man we found. We didn't mention the victim's name, precisely, but the way he spoke about mercenaries in general, I highly doubt someone operating at Mr. Ward's level would have anything to do with someone like that. He said as much."

I groaned again, my hands falling to either side of me, my head falling against the back of the seat. "He laughed in my face about it," I said. "He said there is no such person as Nightmare."

"Which we believe there is," Ronald pressed.

"Exactly," I said, staring at the ceiling above my head. "He said there were other names he had heard that were similar, and said it was nothing more than a means of toying with me. He might as well have called me a fool for falling for it."

Worry tugged at Ronald's face, but he averted his gaze in the rearview mirror.

An eerie silence spread through the car as we drove the rest of the way back to Cousin Richard's. I had no notion of where else we could go. I had no clues, no leads...I had no idea what else to do.

We needed to regroup. I needed a moment to breathe –

More than anything, I needed *not* to stare at the clock as the minutes ticked by. I had no idea how much time I had left, but I knew it wasn't enough to come up with a whole new plan and chase it down before midnight.

Which meant –

I swallowed, but my throat ached. My head throbbed, pain piercing straight through my skull, and behind my eyes.

We arrived at the house far sooner than I expected, which did not bode well for me.

"I'm sorry," Eugene murmured to me as we started inside together. "I allowed my concern to get the better of me, and I should not have made you worry so much. Nor should I have made you feel as if you did anything wrong. You didn't. You did what you could with what we knew. I could have done no better. I am immensely proud of how you carried yourself in that room, under the gaze of a murderer."

I gave him a sidelong glance, but I could not help but

feel a bit of warmth spread through me at his humility. I shook my head, sighing. "I should not have allowed my temper to get the better of me, as I *always* seem to do. It's something Felix used to warn me about, becoming so angry that I can't see clearly."

"It's understandable, given our circumstances," Eugene said.

We passed through the front doors, where Hughes stood by, as if expecting us. "Welcome home, Miss. And good afternoon, sir."

Good afternoon, indeed.

Bitterly, I tried to give him a carefree smile, but it felt wrong. "Hello, Hughes. Is Richard home?" I asked.

"No, unfortunately," Hughes said. "He went out just about an hour ago. He said he would be home in time for dinner, however."

I nodded. Richard's presence wouldn't necessarily change the situation, but I would have preferred the chance to talk with him nevertheless. "Very well. I suppose Mr. Osbourn and I shall retire to the parlor then, for tea."

"Shall I bring coffee, as well?" he asked.

"That would be wonderful, yes," I said.

With a nod and a bow, he turned on his heel and disappeared through the back door.

I sighed, shaking my head. I looked back up at Eugene. "You have always said you wish for me to be candid with you. Well, in regards to visiting Mr. Ward, I must say I am rather displeased about how it seemed you were very much against me. I am unhappier than anyone else about what information Mr. Ward sought about Mr. Edison. While I appreciate your honesty, I wish you would have, in the moment, perhaps been more supportive of – "

Footsteps on the staircase caused my heart to flutter in my chest, and I grimaced, turning around to see Marie coming down the stairs, Gloria right behind her.

"Good afternoon, ladies," Eugene said genially.

"Good afternoon," Marie said.

Gloria's face hardened. "You don't appear to be the triumphant heroes you hoped to be," she said. "I take it Mr. Ward was a dead end?"

"Yes," I said. "Where are you off to?"

"Dorian is coming to pick me up," Gloria said.

"Oswald will be here in a short time, as well," Marie said, her eyes brightening. "Would you care to join us for dinner?"

I hesitated. Normally, I would have no issue accepting, of course, but given the situation –

"You are going to have to eat at some point, Lillian," Eugene said. "And it might not be a bad idea to try and relax, at least for a little while."

Again, I hesitated.

"If anything comes up, I am quite certain they will understand," Eugene added; he must have seen the reservation on my face.

"Of course," Marie said. "We would not want to disrupt the process in any way."

"Very well," I said. "But first I must send a letter."

I turned and started down the hall toward Richard's study, knowing he would have paper and pens that would be easily accessible.

"I'm sorry your errand was unsuccessful," Marie said, starting down the hall after me.

I rolled my eyes, clenching my jaw. I did *not* want to discuss the matter, with her or anyone else right now.

"It was a good guess at the time," Eugene said. "But a bit of a stretch, given what Ward knew."

"It was a very good guess," I retorted, taking a sharp turn into Richard's study. "He was the most likely of the criminals I have faced to this point who would have been capable of such a thing."

"Surely it could have been one of the others," Marie said, walking along beside Eugene as he came in after me.

"I am beginning to think this is a bit more like a secret admirer, as strange as it sounds," Eugene said.

I shot him a look over my shoulder as I approached Richard's desk. "What do you mean?"

"Well, if it isn't someone you've already come into contact with, then it's possible to imagine it is someone who knows what you have done, and what sort of cases you have solved," he said. "Someone who knows enough about you to have concocted such a scheme."

I pulled a sheet of paper from the inside of Richard's desk, and slapped it down on top, with a little more force than I should have. "That's just *grand* then, isn't it?" I asked, rummaging around in the next drawer for a pen. "That could not be *any* more difficult!"

"If Nightmare really considers this to be a game, then he likely would have given you some sort of clue to solve it," Marie said, coming up to the desk, her eyes fixed squarely upon me.

I ignored her as I tried to uncork an inkwell. "Perhaps he did, but it was so vague that I have obviously missed it entirely." The cork wouldn't budge, so I tried to twist it off. "The clues likely had something to do with the victim, but everything we know about him was spelled out in the letter left in his pocket." I chomped down on the cork with my teeth, giving it a good tug before it came unstuck with a satisfying *shlunk!* "He had no family, no friends, and his associates knew very little of him. If Nightmare picked the Sergeant to be a difficult target on purpose, then he is far ahead of me in this game."

I sank down into the chair. Guilt gnawed at my insides. This was the *last* thing I wanted to be doing, knowing precisely what I would have to tell Mr. Edison. I wished more than anything it had been worth it, all the while knowing it hadn't been. All I had managed to do was probably hurt someone...and that troubled me worse than it would have if Mr. Ward had wanted information on *me*.

I grimaced, and twisted the pen, readying it for work.

"So what now?" Marie asked.

"Well...we aren't quite sure," Eugene said. "I think we are going to have to revisit the notes he's written us, and see if there might be some hidden message within them. Lillian, do you have them on you?"

I pulled my satchel over my head and tossed it onto the table. "They're in that front pocket."

Eugene eyed it warily for a moment, but reached out to pull open the clasp.

"I suppose it is the best place to look," Marie said.

I glanced up at her. "You believe this is real and not just a prank combined with a coincidence?" I asked.

She blinked at me, her expression clear. "Of course I do," she said. "I have seen all you have had to endure with these cases in the past. Why would I doubt your expertise now?"

"There are others who are trying to tell me this is nothing more than a joke," I said.

"Then what a wonderful thing that would be," Marie said. "It would mean you won't have to worry about another death happening."

The same thought ate away my insides, but I couldn't quite bring myself to consider the possibility. Not yet. I did not want to give myself false hope.

Eugene read through the letters, passing them back and forth with Marie, who wished for a look at them, too. It gave me a chance to write up a brief note to Mr. Edison, explaining the situation. I apologized profusely, and asked that he forgive me. I had no idea if he even knew who Mr. Ward was, but there had to be some connection there for Mr. Ward to have known about him....apart from me, I hoped.

Not at all satisfied, knowing that he would likely be reading it come this evening, I sealed the envelope and set it aside for Hughes when he stopped to deliver the tea, which he did a short time later.

I cannot worry about Mr. Edison any longer. I have to focus on this. All these distractions are making it nearly impossible to discern the real problem right in front of me.

With another bubble of fear, I began to wonder if this was also not part of Nightmare's plot. I knew logically there was no way he could have predicted something like this, but that didn't mean my mind wasn't working overtime to come up with new and terrible possibilities that might mean my demise.

"Please get this to its recipient as soon as possible," I

urged Hughes as he set down on the desk a tray with the comforting aroma of coffee that brushed against my face. "I will not rest until I know he has received it."

"I shall send it out at once," he said, and made good on his word by hurrying from the room.

"You know..." Marie said, eyeing the letter we'd found in Sergeant McCoy's pocket, her brow furrowed. "Something in this letter seems...off."

"Only one thing?" I asked.

She pursed her lips. "He does seem quite familiar with you, which is slightly odd...but right here, he talks about how he might have done the world a service in killing his victim. It's almost as if he considers himself some sort of...vigilante."

Hope pierced through my fear like streaks of brilliant sunlight through cracks in a window. I straightened as I reached for the coffee. "Go on," I said.

"Yes, it does seem a bit strange, the target he chose," Eugene said. "No one would mourn the victim's death, not really. I am certain those at the inn would have been disconcerted by his death, but likely would not grieve as true friends would."

I considered it as I stirred some fresh, cold cream into the steaming hot liquid, as dark as the mahogany stain on Richard's desk. "That's not a bad observation – "

"Hello, everyone," came a voice near the door.

We all looked over at the same time, and found Oswald striding into the room.

"Darling..." Marie said, hurrying to him.

They greeted one another with a quick murmur between them before he took her hand and the pair started back to us. He quickly searched my face, as well as

Eugene's. "I...take it the search has not gone so well today?"

"Not yet, no," Marie said. "But we might have just stumbled upon something."

"That's good to hear," Oswald said.

I wasn't sure I was *quite* ready to allow myself to hope yet, but I was willing to consider anything at this point.

Oswald looked at Eugene, and his expression hardened slightly. "I am glad to have run into you, though. There's something I need to discuss with you. Would you join me in the hall?"

"Certainly," Eugene said, but I saw worry in his eyes as they strode from the room.

I watched them go, goosebumps rising on my arms. What was that about?

"You know, I wonder if you were to find record of any unexplained deaths within the past month or so, if they would be at all similar to how this Sergeant died," Marie went on, setting the letter down to pour herself some coffee; she'd developed a taste for it, thanks to Felix and I. "Those might be able to give you further clues. Or perhaps at some of the local apothecaries, ask if anyone has come through looking for anything that might be poisonous...though I suppose that is a stretch, isn't it? Practically anything ingested could be lethal in the right amounts."

"I wonder if you weren't closer in regards to a vigilante..." I said. "It might even be to my advantage, if Nightmare is taking out criminals. Why would I need to concern myself with their wellbeing?"

"Precisely," Marie said with a deliberate point of her finger. "His first letter was quite vague, but it seems he has given at least a little more information in the next letter. I believe the incentive he meant, the incentive he assumed would keep you playing, was the death of the Sergeant."

"And any possible deaths that could occur after, yes," I said. "He knows me well enough to see that I will not allow such a crime to stand."

"Well..." She sighed. "The only information he gave you was about the inn, which you went to."

"Right," I said, sipping the coffee. It was still too hot to drink as quickly as I wanted to.

"And you found nothing?"

I shook my head. "I wish I had, but no, we didn't find anything. Chaos erupted in there when they learned about the Sergeant's death, but he was a loner, even there amongst criminals. Hardly anyone knew anything about him."

"So why give you an impossible task?" Marie asked.

I sighed, the overwhelming weight falling back onto my shoulders. "I have no idea...but that is what this is beginning to feel like."

Marie picked up the pair of letters again, examining them side by side, nearly pressing her nose against the paper. "There must be *something* we are missing...something obvious – "

The door to the study opened again, and the gentlemen strolled back inside.

"Is everything all right?" I asked, the worry simply piling upon itself like gravy on a newly filled plate even though I had already eaten my fill.

"Oh, yes," Oswald said in his usual bright, cheery manner. "Just some family business."

"It's nothing to worry about," Eugene said. "It's already being handled."

His words did not entirely dissipate my concerns, but as they came to the desk where Marie and I were having our coffee, it seemed they wished to say no more. As it was their family, I had no place to ask. Not really, anyway.

I gave Eugene a pointed look, which he returned with a small smile before reaching for the slender, silver pitcher that Hughes always served our coffee in.

"Eugene was just telling me that this puzzle is all turning out to be more than we had expected," Oswald said, standing beside Marie, peering at the letters over her shoulder. "I wish there was more we could do. Perhaps Hughes could track down the lad who brought the letter in the first place."

Marie's face lit up. "Oh, darling, that is *brilliant!* I imagine he would be able to find him. Maybe he does know more!"

"I think it's certainly worth trying," Eugene said. "What do you think, Lillian?"

"I am willing to try anything at this point," I said.

We sent for Hughes again, who had just sent Ronald with my letter. He agreed to do as we asked, and hurried to locate the boy.

It took nearly three hours to find him, and then another hour to bring him to the house. When they did, it became clear rather quickly that he knew nothing about his assailant. All he could tell us was that he had been approached in the dark, and that the man had kept his face hidden by a mask, and he wore a dark, hooded cloak to hide his frame. He couldn't even tell us if he was stocky or thin. When I had interrogated the youth for far longer than I should have, I sent him away, annoyed.

By the time I had come back inside and sat down for dinner, it was after nine o'clock.

"The *only* good news I have received today is from Mr. Edison, who sent word after reading my letter that he knew full well who Mr. Ward was, and that he was not at all concerned," I announced. "He said he had protections in place for scum like him, and that Ward could try as he pleased to ruin him, but that it wouldn't work."

"That is good to hear," Eugene said, and I could see some of the tension leave the muscles in his neck and shoulders. "I'll wager you are relieved, as well."

"Yes," I said. "At least I do not have to worry about someone blackmailing him *and* this other nightmare...no humor intended."

Nevertheless, Eugene gave me a bit of a sympathetic smirk.

Richard, who had returned just before I had begun to interrogate the messenger boy, gave me a firm nod. "Good. Let Nightmare realize how seriously you are taking this. I am pleased to see you wasted no time keeping ahead with that."

"Yes, well, it was my own blunder in the first place," I said. "I could have saved myself a great deal of concern had I just kept my mouth shut about Edison."

Richard shrugged. "Sometimes the only way to learn something is by making a mistake. Now you will know how to do better next time."

I frowned, but nodded all the same.

"You've hardly eaten," Eugene said, eyeing my plate.

"He's right," Marie said. "I will not allow you to leave

this table without eating at least *something*. Look at all the work the cook went to for you this evening. Aren't the dill potatoes some of your favorites?"

"Yes, they are," I said, as they were practically the only thing I *had* touched. "I just...do not have much of an appetite."

I glanced up at the clock on the mantle once again.

"Nearly ten..." Richard said. He must have followed my gaze.

Two hours. Were these the last two hours of someone's life, and the only people who knew were sitting around this table...and prowling the streets looking for the target?

"How will you know?" Oswald asked.

"I imagine Nightmare will let me know," I said. I pushed my plate away, the dread in my stomach making everything slosh around uncomfortably. "Why can I not find the answer? I spent all day looking, but I couldn't seem to find anything, or anyone, that could truly help me. What am I missing?"

We had been around this circle nearly a dozen times over the course of the evening, and no one had been able to find a solution. We always came to the same conclusion; we knew nothing about Nightmare himself, apart from the fact that he was a serial killer. He had done a clever job telling me about everything else... apart from himself. And the end goal was to find out who he was, not to learn more about the murdered Sergeant.

We retired to the parlor after dinner. William was sent to bed, though he argued with Richard all the way up the stairs. We sat together and tried to play a game of chess to pass the time, for there was nothing else to be done now.

Midnight chimed, and the entire room sat still, staring at the grandfather clock near the window, moonlight streaking against the glass, pooling at the foot of the ancient timepiece.

As the last *bong* faded into the silence, I shivered. I waited to see what would happen. I didn't know what, but I braced for it.

No one wanted to say what thought was on all our minds; had someone just died?

"Well..." I said in a low voice, breaking the silence.

"What now?" Marie asked.

"I don't know..." I said.

No one wanted to move. Especially me.

"I suppose there will be some more waiting to do...to see if we are in the clear," Eugene said.

I hated that he was right, but I knew he was. Midnight was not the end of this. It might have been just the beginning.

Marie dozed in a chair near the fireplace, and Oswald stared into the fire.

Richard stood near the window, looking out.

Eugene sat with me on the settee, doing nothing apart from being a comfort and a presence to me.

I had no idea what to do. Nothing would distract me, I knew.

It was almost one in the morning when I finally, *finally* began to think that I might be in the clear...when Hughes entered the room.

I could see from the look on his face that the horror I had been waiting for had arrived.

I glanced down at his side, and sure enough, saw a letter clutched in his grasp.

I licked my lips, my mouth going dry. "Who delivered it?"

"No one," he said. "At least, no one that I could see. I heard a knock, and by the time I reached the door, there was no one there. Even after some searching. They managed to get away before I found them. They left this on the doorstep."

Chills raced down my spine as I held out my hand to him.

He placed the letter upon it, and I turned it over, my palms already slick with perspiration. My name stood out plainly on the front, in the same script as the letters before.

With an ever deepening pit in my stomach, I slit the envelope open.

Every eye in the room watched me, or rather, stared at the letter in my hand. I knew it would not be wise to delay. Not reading the words written there would not change what had occurred.

Unfolding it, my eyes nervously swept the page, looking for any particularly frightening words to leap off the page at me –

"What does it say?" Eugene asked, breaking the terrible, trembling silence.

I swallowed, but my throat had tightened so tremendously that I felt I could barely breathe. "It...it's just two sentences..." I said. "*Watch for the paper tomorrow morning. Same rules apply as before. You will have until midnight to find me.*"

Marie looked over at Oswald, eyes wide, hand

clutched to her mouth. He looked hardly better, with a pale expression and wide, nervous eyes.

Eugene took a step toward me. "May I see the letter?"

I nodded, numbly, and handed it to him.

Richard approached, gazing at the letter over Eugene's shoulder. His brow wrinkled as he looked at me. "I imagine it will be one of the names in the obituary section…" he said.

A flood of guilt crashed against me, making my knees weak. I sank down onto the bench behind me, the shadows alongside the fireplace engulfing me.

How could I not have taken this more seriously?

"I suppose we have our answer…" Eugene said. "This Nightmare is doing exactly as he said he would."

I turned my face to him. "How many more people is he going to kill?" I asked. "How much longer before I can find out who he is?"

No one quite knew what to say, and as such, they gave me some space as I gave in to despair for a while. Eugene remained nearby, while I paced back and forth before the dying embers of the fireplace.

Sleep did not even tempt me. The hours passed, and before I knew it, dawn had come.

Wordlessly, I hurried to the foyer, Eugene coming along beside me. I waited there for Hughes, knowing that the post would be delivered at seven thirty, sharp, as it was every morning.

Hughes thanked the delivery boy with a polite smile… but it faded as soon as he shut the door behind him, eyeing me with apprehension.

He crossed over and handed the newspaper to me,

before turning to make his way to the dining room with the rest of the mail.

My heart thundered in my chest, making me nauseous. I flipped open to the obituaries...but found none.

I blinked at the page, my foggy, tired mind not moving as quickly as it normally did.

"Maybe it's in with the reported crimes?" Eugene suggested.

"Oh...right..." I said. I turned to that page.

After a few frustrating moments, I let out a groan.

"Do you see anything?" I asked.

"There..." Eugene said, prodding the top, right corner with his finger.

It was a small section, but at once I could see he was right.

A young woman was found dead at Warrington Theatre in the early hours of the morning. Foul play is suspected, given the grisly scene.

I looked up at Eugene, my stomach twisting, and determination solidifying.

"This is it," I said, smacking the paper with the back of my hand. "It has to be."

"Then let's be on our way," Eugene said, reaching for the coats on the coat rack. "We have no time to lose."

8

"The victim is Miss Freya Samuels, a world-class ballerina," I read some time later. "Born and raised in Cambridge, she began to study dance at the young age of three. She demonstrated a natural grace and poise that immediately elevated her above her peers, and was selected to appear in a performance of Othello before she had reached the age of ten."

"An impressive history," Eugene said. "It's a shame she met such a terrible end..."

He gazed past the paper I held, down at the poor girl at our feet.

It was almost beautiful, in a way. Perhaps poetic was a better term, as there was such a sharp contrast between her silky white leotard and skirt, her perfect bun tied up so neatly in a matching snowy white ribbon at the back of her head...and the crimson blood that speckled her body like the dots on a robin's egg.

I sighed, kneeling down beside her.

She had exquisite skin, flawlessly smooth, free of all

blemishes. Her hair, as blonde as starlight, shone in the bright lights of the theater that glared done upon her from overhead. The way she lay there, I might have thought she had simply fallen asleep on the main stage after a long practice. She seemed almost peaceful.

The wound across her stomach told me otherwise, however. It was long and deep, and I didn't allow my gaze to linger there too long in hopes of *not* seeing more than I would have liked. Blood had blossomed out, up her chest and down toward her hips. It had pooled beneath her, some of it having seeped into the cracks between the floorboards.

According to the police we had met guarding the entrance, the body and the scene remained mostly untouched, just as they had been found. Luckily, one of those officers had recognized my name from a mention of one of my cases in the newspaper, and they had agreed to allow us a few minutes to examine the body.

"She must have been caught when she was leaving last night," Eugene said, breaking into my thoughts.

"I imagine so..." I said. "That is what the director said, at least. They were having the final performance of whatever show it was..." I couldn't think clearly enough to remember the show's name, not after a stressful night of no sleep. "But she is still wearing her costume. Nightmare must have managed to grab her before she even reached her dressing room..."

The theater was well known, though small and supposedly a place where young talent went to gain exposure, hopefully providing them with an opportunity to be seen by directors of more prominent theaters. It was in a beautiful location, alongside the river with stunning views of the skyline of the city across the water.

Entirely different from the cemetery where we had found the Sergeant, that was for certain.

"What do you suspect the connection with her is?" I asked Eugene. "The paper said her last name was Samuels?" I pulled it out from under my arm, reading through it again. "I see no resemblance to the dead Sergeant."

"Maybe she is a daughter he never knew he had..." Eugene said.

"A bit of a long shot, but I suppose it's possible," I said. "Nightmare told us he had no family, and no friends."

"He never specified if it was family he knew of or not," Eugene said. "He does seem very intentional with how he words things."

"Maybe..." I said, though doubt prevented me from considering it much further than that.

"There's no letter..." Eugene said, stepping around the tacky pool of blood toward her head. "I think he would have made it obvious."

"There's nowhere to hide one..." I said, eyeing her tight costume. It left little to the imagination.

"Let's begin with what we know," Eugene said. "We can almost pinpoint the time she was killed last night."

"Around midnight, as per Nightmare's rules," I said.

"Right, which matches up with what the director told us when we arrived," Eugene said. "The performance ended at half past eleven. Someone found her just before one in the morning."

I nodded. "That is one certainty..." I said. "Though not terribly helpful. It means that it could have been any one of the attendees, or any of the cast. That could be hundreds of people."

"That must have been Nightmare's intention all along..." Eugene mused.

I grimaced. "He certainly isn't making this *easy* for us, is he?" I asked, walking around the other side of the girl.

Her costume was so delicate and so beautiful. It shimmered slightly, like freshly fallen snow. Her pale skin, now almost the same color, must have been lovely and rosy.

"She can't be older than...what...eighteen, would you say?" I asked.

"I thought younger..." Eugene said.

I frowned, shaking my head. "This whole thing is just...just despicable," I said, opening the paper once again. "There is nothing here that really helps us. It tells us about *her,* not about Nightmare."

"There has to be an obvious clue here," Eugene said. "Maybe it's something with the timing of their deaths? Or maybe some sort of similarity between them?"

"They could not be more opposite," I said. "Even the way they died is entirely different. He was poisoned. She was stabbed." My nose wrinkled. "I think I would have preferred to go out as he did..."

Eugene's face paled.

"What else could we be missing? He was a criminal, she a performer. He dealt with people's problems, she entertained the masses. He had lived a long, hard life, and she had barely begun hers. Apart from the fact that they both became targets for Nightmare, what else do they share?"

"Well...didn't Marie suggest that Nightmare might

consider himself some sort of vigilante? What if this young woman had some sort of sordid past or dealings?" Eugene asked.

I scratched at my chin. "That might not be a bad thought," I said. "Perhaps she had only the appearance of perfection. She could be the best of her profession and yet have dark secrets in her personal life..."

"What else did the paper say about her?" Eugene asked, coming back to stand beside me.

"Not a great deal..." I said, gazing down at the article again. "It seems that her father is a prominent business-man, and his wife the daughter of a marquis."

"Well, at least her parents are alive," Eugene said, brows rising. "I think it would be wise to go and speak with them, next."

"I agree," I said. "Coming to see her here might have been nothing more than a waste of time. We have learned nothing from seeing her. We might as well have just gone straight to them."

"We didn't know that at the time, though," Eugene said.

"That is precisely how this *whole* affair has gone, hasn't it?" I asked. "We always learn things *after* we have made the mistake and wasted the time."

"Do not be too hard on yourself," Eugene said. "We did learn something this time, and it's how she died. That, and I still cannot believe Nightmare wouldn't have wanted you to see something with both of these deaths. There has to be something that just hasn't clicked yet."

"And how many more of these sorts of scenes do we have to see before it does click?" I asked, glaring up at him.

"Hopefully no more," he said, undeterred by my frustration. At least he knew I wasn't upset with him.

"Yes, hopefully not," I said. I looked down at the poor girl again, sighing. "Is there anything else here for us?"

"I don't know," Eugene said.

"Nor do I."

I chewed the inside of my lip, surveying the entirety of the scene around me, trying to make some sense of it.

"Something isn't sitting right," I said, and a flutter of fear began to worm its way into the already saturated worry that had been plaguing me for days. "This kill is nothing at all like the first one. You don't suppose..." The thought bubbled to the surface, and I could not smother it fast enough. "That this was *not* done by Nightmare?"

Eugene looked back down at the girl.

"There was no specification in the letter," I said. I reopened the paper for what felt like the hundredth time, my eyes passing over the page. "All he told us was to look at today's paper. We *assumed* that it was her, but what if it wasn't?"

I poured over the reported crimes, reading them as quickly as I could, one by one.

Eugene came to my side, and read along with me.

"...Theft on Prince Edward Avenue...another robbery at a jewelry store...assault near the harbor...a drunkard arrested for public indecency – " I grimaced, flipping to the back where the obituaries were. "Maybe we missed them. Maybe they're in a different place on Saturdays – "

No matter how much I looked, though, I couldn't find anything.

"She is the only death," Eugene said, glancing at her, his face falling. "Which...is tragic."

I knew he was thinking it was good that only one death had occurred, both for us and for the overall well-being of the city...but then when he stopped to *really* consider what that meant...

"The only thing..." I said, studying the way the victim lay once again, taking a full circle around her, my mind working. I studied the way she had been so casually draped across the stage, her arms so relaxed at her side, her pointed shoes tied in ribbons so elegantly crossed at the ankles..."The *only* thing I can think is that the both of them seem to have been positioned in an almost poetic way. He was laid on an unmarked grave, she on the stage as if acting out one of her performances."

"That's quite abstract, but I believe you are on to something there," Eugene said. "It is almost like a reflection of their lives, in a way. They both made a statement. They were obviously placed in these locations."

"Right," I said.

A knot tightened in my chest, and I glanced at Eugene. A deal of time had passed while we were here. We had been barred by the police at first, and then got caught up talking to the director who had been more concerned about his own wellbeing than that of the victim. Then we had stood here for nearly an hour. "What time is it?" I asked Eugene.

Eugene pulled back his sleeve, eyeing his watch. The slight rise of his brows told me that we had spent far too much time here already. "Noon," he said.

I gaped at him. "Noon? What in the world – how did we – "

A sudden noise at the back of the theater sent a

shockwave through me as if I'd been struck by a bolt of lightning.

I whipped around, the brilliant light above stinging my eyes as I tried to look into the blackness behind the last row of seats. I pressed my hand to my brow, shielding my eyes from as much of the light as I could.

"Hello?" Eugene called, taking a step toward the edge of the stage. "Who's there?"

There was no answer...but a movement near the far right door caught my eye as my vision adjusted to the dark.

I turned just in time to see the swish of a black cloak flying out of the room.

"That's him!" I cried, leaping off the stage. "That's Nightmare!"

9

My knees buckled as I made contact with the ground. It was much farther than I had anticipated when I had unthinkingly jumped off the edge of the theater stage. The shadows deceptively congregated around the front row of velvet seats, so by the time I had realized my mistake, it was far too late to remedy it.

I fell over, stretching my arms out in front of me as my knees slammed into the ground. It didn't matter that it was carpeted; pain shot through all four of my limbs as I rolled to the side.

"Lillian!" Eugene cried. I heard another thud beside me, and his face, haloed in brilliant light, appeared over my own a moment later, looking stricken. "Are you all right?"

I grimaced, hoping I hadn't broken something.

"Can you move?" he asked.

I stretched out my legs beneath me, and while a sharp

pain seared white hot, it had already begun to dull. I did the same for my arms, and wiggled all ten of my fingers.

"I...I think so," I said. I stared up the aisle, which seemed far steeper from where I lay on the floor. "We have to catch him! I am *not* losing him! Not now!" I reached out for Eugene. "Help me up, please!"

"Of course," Eugene said, and he swept me off the ground and onto my feet. He gave me a moment to steady myself, secure in his grasp. "Good?"

My knees felt shaky, but it could have been the adrenaline surging through me. "As good as I will be," I said.

I tentatively started up the aisle, toward the door, knowing I had already lost precious seconds. He could have gotten away by now! With that thought, I picked up my pace, my gaze fixed upon that back door.

I burst through it, looking all around. I found myself in a side hall off the theater; one end leading to the main foyer, where I could hear the dull murmur of conversation between the police and some of the staff, and down the other –

"This way!" I exclaimed, hurrying toward another door at the end of the hall. "I could swear I just saw that shut!"

Eugene, with his long legs so much like Felix's, hurried past me to the door. He threw himself against it when I was only two thirds of the way there, and stumbled outside into the grey light of the afternoon.

He turned left and then right. He gave a sudden shout, and took off out of my sight.

My heart slammed even harder against my ribs, turning my stomach as I reached the door. *Eugene, be careful!*

I went out through the door...only to find myself on a metal, grated walkway. My shoes slipped against the smooth surface, and I grabbed for the narrow railing just across from the door. Whirling around, I heard the consistent *clang, clang, clang* of footsteps above me. I looked up just in time to see the bottom of Eugene's feet passing over the metal steps just above my head; the staircase he'd taken wrapped around its self as it ascended, keeping close to the exterior wall of the theater.

I started up the stairs after him, hoping against all hope that we had not missed our chance, that in my stupidity and impulsiveness, I had not lost the only chance I had, wasted the opportunity to get ahead and take advantage of my enemy's mistake.

What had he been doing back there, lurking in the shadows? Why had he been watching us? How overconfident did he have to be to so blatantly stand in the same room as us? With a sick pang in the pit of my stomach, I wondered if he thought himself so invincible that he would just sit back and watch us flounder about?

I grimaced, and rounded another corner of the staircase.

Eugene's clanging footsteps faded, and I knew he must have reached the top, wherever that was. A quick glance over my head told me I only had two more sets of stairs to go, and I began to take them two at a time.

I reached the top just a few moments after Eugene did. It landed us up on the roof of the theater, a flat, long, narrow stretch of tiles, with a row of five or six air vents, steam filtering out into the cold, autumn air.

A figure was at the end of the roof, standing up on the

brick ledge, a black cloak draped over his shoulders concealing him entirely. A dark hood shielded his face in shadow, and it struck me how much shorter he was than I had expected.

I took a step forward. "We've got you, Nightmare," I said, trying to slow my frantic breathing. "You can't go anywhere from here."

Nightmare said nothing, simply stood there.

"You did this to yourself, you know," I said, starting toward him, my fingers itching to reach for my hidden knives.

"You underestimated us...or perhaps overestimated your own success. You thought you would be able to stand there and watch, perhaps find yourself amused at our progress. But you are only human, which I am pleased to see."

Still he said nothing. He remained perfectly still, apart from the flutter of his cloak as the wind rushed around him.

"If you had just left us your...gift, and been on your way, then you wouldn't have found yourself in this predicament – "

Before the words had even left my mouth, Nightmare jumped off the roof backward, spreading his arms out, his cloak splaying out all around him like the wings of a bat. He pulled his knees up just as gravity took hold of him, dragging him down toward the earth below.

Two full heartbeats passed as I stared at him in horror. Did he jump to his death?

Eugene and I both raced to the edge.

I grabbed tight to the side before leaning over, just in time to see a sizable *splash* in the river below. How had I forgotten? All the running through the theater, up the side of the building...I had lost my orientation, my sense of direction. Why had I not stopped to consider this?

"I wonder if he survived that fall..." Eugene murmured, his eyes fixed on the water below.

I realized we had not yet seen him surface. I stared at the murky, steel grey water, looking for any sign of movement beneath the surface. Surely, with all that heavy clothing and the thick cloak, he'd be dragged down, sodden in the water. "I don't see him," I said.

"We should go check," Eugene said. "If we can grab him before he manages to get out of the river, then we can put a stop to all this once and for all."

"Right," I said, and hope flared within me. I had been dragged through an emotional see-saw within the past few minutes alone, between seeing him standing in the back, falling off the stage, chasing him up the stairs, and then him jumping –

For the first time since all this started, I began to feel as if we had a chance. A *real* chance.

"It's obvious he panicked," I mused as we hurried away, back down the stairs as fast as our legs could carry us. It had begun to rain and the metal was quickly becoming slick in the drizzle. "That's why he jumped like he did."

"It was insanity, that's what it was," Eugene said over his shoulder, trying to be careful as well. "It seems the possibility of death by landing in the wrong place was preferable to being caught."

"That does seem bizarre," I said. "He did not think we'd see him, standing back there in the dark."

"No, he didn't," Eugene said. "As you said, that

reminds us he is human, and therefore, we can beat him. He didn't anticipate us being able to best him. He was too arrogant."

The hope grew deeper within me. "This is good."

"It will be good if we can catch him," Eugene said as he reached the bottom flight of stairs, the door back into the theater coming into sight at the far end of the walkway. "Otherwise..."

I had no interest in considering the alternative.

We hurried back through the theater, and found a side door that led out into the alleyway. I followed Eugene through the door, down the lane, and toward the river that ran along the back side of the theater. My heart pounded. We were so close! If we could just catch him!

"Do you see anything?" I asked, unable to stop myself.

"Not yet..." Eugene said, slowing as he reached the edge. The river butted up against the road, separated by a simple, stone wall. The water lapped up against the wall a short distance below.

"The water is too muddy..." I said, the poignant hope quickly fading, like a pricked balloon. "How are we supposed to see anything in there?"

Not only that, but the river was much wider than I had realized; up atop the building, it hadn't seemed so far to the other side, but standing beside it, I could see how vast of a distance it was.

"I don't imagine he could have gotten very far," Eugene said, his hardened gaze sweeping up both sides of the wall.

"How do you feel about splitting up to look?" I asked, already starting down along the narrow pass between the back of the building and the river.

"Not good," Eugene said. "That would be deeply unwise. What if he is lying in wait for us?"

I frowned. "I had not considered that," I said. "Fine. Let's just start looking."

"This is about where he landed..." Eugene said, pointing down a ways. He guided me over there, careful to allow me the chance to navigate broken bits of the stone wall and other debris that had accumulated behind the theater. I saw more than my fair share of broken glass bottles, likely from one too many drunkards lying about after or during a show.

"Yes," I said. "And I can't say that I am exactly surprised he is gone, but it doesn't make me terribly happy to see he's disappeared."

"Nor I..." he said. "But look here. There are wet spots along the wall."

"Could he have pulled himself out?" I asked.

Eugene's face fell as he approached the wall with caution. "There's a ladder here."

My heart sank. "Really?"

"I am beginning to wonder if this was not a planned stunt," Eugene said, turning his face up to the top of the theater. I followed suit, thinking with a pit in my stomach about the metal staircases we had raced up and down. They weren't on this side of the building, of course, but seeing the top of the building made me realize just how high we had been...and how far Nightmare had jumped.

"You really think he would have calculated his ability to survive that far of a fall?" I asked. "That's...well, that's insanity, is what it is."

"You have no argument from me," Eugene said,

frowning up at the rooftop. "But what if he meant for us to see him?"

A horrified knot tightened in my chest, breathing new life into the paralyzing idea that Nightmare really just might be that much better than I was at all this. I shook my head, forcefully shoving the thoughts aside. "No, there's no way," I said. "We cornered him, and he did the only thing he could. There is no way anyone would willingly jump this far. Not unless he scouted the area before and knew the water would be deep enough. I just can't believe that."

"Can't believe it? Or don't want to?" Eugene asked.

I looked away, looking up and down the river. There had been no movement, not on the street, behind any of the buildings, or in the river itself. There was no indication, apart from some wet spots along the wall, that indicated our foe was anywhere around.

There was no way he could have held his breath for this long, and my only hope was that he had knocked his head on something under the water and then became trapped somehow. A slim chance, but...

I shot Eugene a glare, planting my hands on my hips. "Fine. Let's say he *did* plan this," I relented. "Then what? We just give up and go home, because there would be no way for us to find him? If he did plan this, then he was *toying* with us, and if that's the case – "

"If that's the case, then we have our work cut out for us," Eugene said, his brow furrowing as he regarded me. "This isn't the end. He isn't unbeatable, as your panic might be suggesting that he is. He *is* human, just as you told him – "

"Fat lot of good that did me," I said, rolling my eyes.

"Talking to him like I knew what he was doing, like I was the one in control – "

"Lillian, he might be a few steps ahead, but that doesn't mean that he – "

"He *escaped* Eugene!" I cried. "He's *gone!* We may as well have lost now!"

Eugene blinked at me, startled by my sudden burst of rage. "Why? Are we not in the same place that we were this morning?" he asked.

"No!" I exclaimed. "He was *so close,* I should have just grabbed him off the wall, or thrown one of my knives at his chest – this could have been done, Eugene, over right there on the roof! But instead I allowed myself a moment to gloat, to relish in what I assumed was his defeat."

"You cannot chide yourself for errors of the past," Eugene said. "And if he planned for us to follow him, then he wouldn't have let you get close to him, anyway. You will drive yourself mad if you stand here and think of all the ways you can punish yourself."

I balled my hands into fists and stomped away from him.

He was right, and I knew it full well. I just didn't want to admit it.

I stopped on the road once again, at the corner where it snaked around the side of the theater and passed by along the river. I pinched the bridge of my nose, drawing in gulps of the scummy river air, willing my heart to slow.

"I'm sorry," I said in a low voice as I heard his foot-steps behind me. "I didn't mean to lash out at you. Again."

Eugene appeared in front of me, and he gave me a

small, half-moon smile. "I understand," he said. "But I am not your enemy. You must remember that."

"I know," I snapped, and then sighed. "I know full well."

I looked all around. "I just keep hoping he is going to appear, walk out into the open so we can get him."

"That would be convenient for us, but not likely," he said.

"Well...now what do we do?" I asked. "There wasn't anything particularly interesting about him. Black cloak, black hood, no visible face..."

"I did see some red," Eugene said. "At least, I thought I did...when he was running away from me up the stairs."

"Where?" I asked.

"I don't know, it was just a flash," he said. "A narrow strip of some sort. Around his wrist, I believe."

It would make sense that I hadn't seen that, given the fact the only time I *had* seen him had been when he was standing still, obscured by his cloak fully closed around him. I shook my head. "That doesn't tell us anything, apart from the fact that he seems not to exclusively wear black." I wrinkled my nose. "He was shorter than I imagined."

"I thought the same," he said.

"Anything else?" I asked.

Eugene shook his head. "He wore simple riding boots, leather gloves...nothing distinctive."

"This is positively infuriating," I said, rubbing my temple, putting pressure on the tender skin. "When he was standing right in front of us, we still could not manage to learn anything new."

"No...but that doesn't mean we have no hope," he said.

"You are quite optimistic," I scoffed.

"Perhaps I am," he said. "But I think it's better than allowing myself to be pessimistic about it."

I glared at him. Felix would have said something similar, I knew. Maybe Eugene knew that, too.

"It seems so strange to me that he just...stood there in the back, watching us," I said. A shiver raced down my spine. "It's disturbing, really."

"I have not wanted to admit it out loud, but I've wondered if he has been watching us a lot of the time," Eugene said in a murmur. "There would be no way to know for sure, of course, but I have suspected it all along."

"I have as well," I said.

As if I might catch him peeking around a corner, staring at us, I took a quick look around.

"Which makes me think he will be watching us again...right?" I asked.

Eugene nodded. "I imagine he will be. He might even be right now."

Which meant that I needed to keep my idea to myself, then. At least until we were in the car and I could know for certain we were alone.

If this was true, then Nightmare would not go far. I could almost be sure of that. If he wanted to see how everything played out, then he might watch to see where we went next, follow up, and make it seem as if he had known we would do what we did all along.

If he *was* watching us, then maybe he wasn't as far ahead of us as I had thought.

"Maybe you are right," I said. "Maybe we will be able to find him again."

Eugene nodded, but I could see the renewed worry in his gaze. Maybe the same thoughts had passed through his mind. I would know soon enough.

He and I agreed to head back to the car then, and on to the next part of our journey.

My determination hardened as we walked. We would need to be more aware of our surroundings going forward, as our enemy could be lurking anywhere. Really, he could be anyone and we wouldn't recognize him.

Instead of allowing worry to overwhelm me, I forced myself to consider the reality; he would give himself away again. He would make a mistake somewhere, some way. There had to be a clue that we were missing, and soon, there might be another death to provide another.

I grimaced, but knew that it was true.

If he was watching, which I had to assume he was, then it might be possible to force his hand, to act in a way he would *not* expect. That might mean finding a way to bait him into coming out into the open.

The only question was...what could we possibly do that would convince him to leave the comfort of the shadows?

10

"We only have one choice," I said as Ronald closed the door to the car behind me with a resounding *shlunk*. "And that's to go visit the family of the murdered ballerina."

"That's what I thought you'd say," Eugene said. "And was my own assumption as well. I am glad we had the foresight to ask the director where they lived."

I eyed the sidewalk just outside the window, gazing into the faces of those that passed by the car. There were quite a few people for this time of day, but as this was a prominent entertainment district in the city, and it was getting closer to evening, I had little reason to be surprised. Still, the thought that any one of these people passing by could be Nightmare ate at me. One couple passed right by the car, arm in arm, he grinning the stupid grin of love, and she tossing her golden curls over her shoulder as she laughed happily.

My stomach turned as another emotion, a much different feeling, washed over me.

I was…jealous.

I glanced at Eugene, who turned as he felt my gaze. He gave me a gentle smile, and reached across the distance between us to lay his hand atop mine.

That should be us, walking around without a care, with a full night of shows and dinner to look forward to.

It didn't seem fair that we had just left the scene of a murder, the blood barely begun to dry on the poor girl's body, ready to go and speak with her parents. What a *joy* this was going to be.

"Are you all right?" Eugene asked, studying my face.

I gave him a smile in return, but it might as well have been a grimace for as much happiness as it contained. "Just…thinking," I said. I didn't need to expound on my thoughts. Not right now, at least.

I smoothed my dress over my knees, and tried to breathe deeply. *There will be time for those things later, after this is over.*

After this is over.

At the moment, that seemed like an impossibility. What if it never did end?

Ronald pulled his own door shut a moment later, turning to look over his seat at us. "Where to next, Miss?" he asked.

Eugene gave him the directions, and we were off.

"Now that we are out of earshot, is there anything we must discuss?" I asked.

Eugene shifted in his seat, but Ronald spoke first, his thick brows furrowing in the reflection of the mirror.

"Out of earshot?" he asked. "What's been going on?"

"We nearly caught Nightmare," Eugene said. "Found

him spying on us at the back of the theater when we were investigating."

Ronald's eyes widened, and he nearly hit the car in front of us. He quickly slammed on the brake pedal, his head snapping forward. "Spying on you?" he asked after the other car slowly pulled farther away, and he started off once more.

"Yes," I said, and I gave him a quick account. "We are wondering if he's been watching us every bit of the way." I glanced at Eugene. "I'm sure he was there at the cemetery with us."

He nodded. "And likely in the inn, too."

Goosebumps appeared on my arms as I considered that.

"Though, I don't think he has been in your cousin's home at all," Eugene said.

My head whipped around. "You don't think he could have infiltrated the staff – "

"No," Eugene said. "No, I very much doubt that."

"Why?" I asked.

"Because there's been no one new hired, for starters," Ronald said, glancing at us briefly from the mirror. "And if anyone had started acting suspicious, someone would have said something."

My eyes narrowed. "You think everyone is so loyal to Richard?"

Ronald nodded. "Of course," he said with conviction. "I have no doubt. He's earned the respect that he gets, and anyone who has ever stepped out of line was either promptly fired or whipped into shape. You needn't worry."

"What if a long-time employee decided to do this?" I asked.

"That would likely be even more obvious to your cousin," Eugene said. "As Ronald said, they're all loyal to him. If that changed, it would be noticeable."

I chewed on the inside of my lip. Suddenly, it felt as if nowhere was safe.

"Take heart, Miss," Ronald said. "You got close to catching him today. I reckon you're close, now. Maybe this family will be able to tell you what you need to know."

"Yes, but how will we get information without Nightmare hearing of it?" I asked.

Eugene scratched his ear, his gaze distant for a moment. "Well...the easy answer would be to ensure that the door is closed, and we are the only people in the room."

Ronald nodded. "And I can watch the front of the house, make sure no one goes in. Could be he poses as a postman, or some such."

"Right, because we have no idea what he looks like," I said.

"Well...apart from the fact that he isn't very tall," Eugene said. "Not that it's terribly helpful, but we will be able to distinguish that at least those taller than you, Lillian, are not a possibility."

"While it's a good observation, it isn't *precisely* helpful," I said. "We have gone from narrowing down from absolutely everyone to now perhaps three quarters of those whom we see."

Eugene shrugged. "It's a start."

I sighed. "I guess the best part about that whole run-in is that now we can better prepare ourselves. He cannot see inside our minds, can he?"

"Exactly," Eugene said. "And if we can ensure there are no listening ears around..."

"Then maybe we have a chance," I said.

"Yes," Eugene agreed.

Beginning to feel a bit more hopeful, Eugene and I reviewed what we had seen at the theater. Ronald made a very astute observation as we drew closer to the girl's home; her death happened less than five miles from the Sergeant's. It wasn't much to go on, but it might have some meaning. I began to wonder if Nightmare lived in that part of the city. It would explain why he was able to make the kills the way he had, and at the time he had. It would also explain his familiarity with the area, wouldn't it? I chewed on the matter, feeling once again that I might have slightly more control, a little better handle on the situation in general.

The home of the girl was in a prominent neighborhood not far from Hyde Park. Each and every house stood in perfect little rows, all matching the next, with the same pristine windows, the same sparkling clean exteriors. The family's front door, cherry red, had been fixed with a black bow...a symbol that really could only mean one thing.

My heart sank as we passed by it. Twenty-four hours ago, this door would not have held so morbid a decoration...

"Mr. Samuels?" I asked as Eugene and I were escorted into a dimly lit parlor at the back of the astoundingly beautiful townhome. "My name is Miss Lillian Crawford, and I am here to help you and your family find out who killed your daughter."

It seemed that I had not learned as much tact as I should have, because poor Mrs. Samuels, a perfect reflection of the ballerina with the same hair seemingly made of glittering starlight, burst into tears and hid her face away.

Mr. Samuels, slim and tall sitting beside his wife, must have been where his daughter had received her slender form fit for dancing. He glared at me as his wife cried into his shoulder, his arm wrapped firmly around her. "I don't believe I ever asked the police to send us a detective."

"The police did not send me," I said. "I have come on my own behalf. You see, I am investigating a case, and – "

Mrs. Samuels' cries drowned out the rest of my thought.

"No," Mr. Samuels said with a firm shake of his head. "No, I am sorry, but we have no interest in your kind. All it will do is cause us further heartache, and we have had enough for all eternity."

This was not going the way I had expected.

"Mr. Samuels, your daughter's death is unfortunately part of a string of murders that have happened in this city, and it would be – " My eyes darted to the window when a fluttering motion caught my eye. My heart nearly stopped, as all I could think about was Nightmare's cloak.

A window stood open, letting the bitter wind inside.

The room was stuffy, certainly, and could have probably used the crisp air.

I hurried over to it and slammed the window shut.

"What was that for?" Mr. Samuels barked. "Listen here, you cannot just – "

"Mr. Samuels, it is *very* important that you listen to me for a moment," I said. "Just a moment. If after you have heard what I have to say, you still wish for me to leave, then I will. But this is bigger than the death of your daughter, as horrendous and tragic as it was."

He glared at me, his wife apparently unaware of the conversation we were having.

Eugene, however, moved to close the door behind him.

"What – how dare you!" Mr. Samuels said, color rising in his face. "You – are you the ones that – "

"No, sir," I said, pulling the drapes closed on the window for good measure. If my theory was true, and Nightmare learned as much as we did by spying on us when we had these conversations, then we needed all the advantage we could acquire. "No, we are not the ones who killed your daughter. But we do know who did...sort of."

Mr. Samuels grimaced, his salt and pepper moustache quivering above his thin lips. "I do not care to be toyed with, Miss Crawford. I suggest that you make your intentions known within the next few minutes or you will be thrown out..."

"Very well," I said. "I am a private detective, and I have been following the case of a serial killer." There was no real need to tell him that Nightmare was treating this whole affair as a game, directed at me, as it was not entirely helpful when it came to the death of his daughter. He needed facts, not to be further burdened with my concerns. "He calls himself Nightmare, and your daughter was his second victim."

Mr. Samuels' grimace gave way to shock, his eyes widening. "...Second?" he murmured.

I nodded. "Yes. There was another the night before, right around the same time, just a few miles from here. Now, I need to ask you some questions about your daughter, as well as anything you might know about the other victim, as any information you give us could lead us to Nightmare's whereabouts."

His face darkened once more. "You said you knew who he was," he said.

"I have seen him, but I do not yet know his identity," I said. "He has been leaving a trail of letters in his wake, as clues."

"Why did he kill my daughter?" Mr. Samuels asked, his voice cracking. "Why did he kill my Freya?"

"I...don't know yet, Mr. Samuels," I said as gently as I could. "But I promise that I am going to do all I can to find out the reason why."

Mr. Samuels tried to gather himself, running his hand over the whole of his face as if to wipe away the memories of the past day he was certainly reliving over and over again. "The police said they would do what they could, but there was so little evidence. They suspected it to be some sort of beggar, or perhaps a cutpurse." He shook his head. "How would they have gotten into the theater? They have never had an issue with people wandering in; it's always very well protected." He laid a hand on the knee of his wife, who simply sat there beside him, her head in her hands. "This whole thing...it just has not felt right."

"That's because something was amiss," I said. "I don't know why she was targeted, but I aim to find out."

Mr. Samuels eyed Eugene, who stood patiently beside him. He frowned. "You're that famous pianist, aren't you?"

"Eugene Osbourn, sir, and yes," Eugene said.

Mr. Samuels' forehead wrinkled further. "I remember you played for one of the performances that Freya danced in a few years ago...She had only a minor part, I doubt you would remember." He glanced at me. "And you are now working with a private detective?"

"We're engaged, sir," I said, jumping in to protect Eugene. "He has agreed to help me for that very reason you mentioned. He does remember, and it troubles him to know something so horrific has happened."

It was a lie, but if it would encourage them to help us, then it needed to be said.

The look on Eugene's face told me he understood what I was doing. We didn't have a great deal of time left; a glance at a clock on the wall informed me we had less than six hours, in fact, before another death was to occur.

And that is entirely avoiding the emotional implications of throwing around words like "engaged"...

I tried not to think about how that might have caused more discomfort for the both of us than I had stopped to consider.

Mr. Samuels thought for a long, hard minute. Apart from the last statement, we had no reason to lie to him. I truly did want to help them. More than any other death that I had investigated, I felt personally responsible for the ballerina's death. If I had solved this the day before, then she would still be here.

The thought made my stomach ache, bile rising in the back of my throat.

"I want to make this monster pay for what he did," I said. "He deserves anything that the authorities decide for so heinous a crime."

Mr. Samuels swallowed hard, his jaw clenching. "Very well," he said. "What can we do to help you?"

Good. At least we had managed to convince him. "First questions first, I suppose. Have you ever heard of this man who calls himself Nightmare?" I asked.

Mr. Samuels shook his head, smoothing his moustache with the ends of his fingers. "No..." he said. "Until you mentioned it, I never heard such a name."

A long shot, I had known, but worth trying. "Very well. What about Sergeant McCoy?"

I did not want to give any sort of clue as to who he was, or what connection he had, hoping Mr. Samuels would be able to dig something out of his memory that could help us. The last thing I needed was to waste more time chasing ourselves in circles with information that we already knew full well.

"No...I cannot say I know that name either," Mr. Samuels said. "I am familiar with another Sergeant, but I have never heard of a McCoy."

I glanced at Eugene, who returned my gaze with a questioning look.

How should we proceed? What would be the best step forward?

"Very well," I said. "I thought it might be too good to be true, but I had to ask all the same."

"Who is he?" Mr. Samuels asked.

"He was the other victim," I said. "And I wanted to know if there might have been a connection between him and your family."

"And?" Mr. Samuels asked.

I shook my head. "There's very little we know about him; no family, no friends. He was quite alone. This doesn't help, as there were no leads to follow."

"But then you found us," Mr. Samuels said.

"Yes," I said. "Which leads me to question you now. Mr. Samuels, is there anyone who might have had reason to target your daughter in this manner? A jilted lover, perhaps? Or maybe a betrayed friend? Or perhaps even a colleague that she outstripped who became jealous?"

Mr. Samuels shook his head, his expression darkening. "She was perhaps the sweetest young woman one could have known. She was quiet, which is what drew her to dancing in the first place. She always told us that it spoke *for* her..."

He hung his head as his wife's sobs began anew.

"I'm...I'm sorry," he said, pulling a handkerchief from the cuff of his sleeve, dabbing at his eyes. "This is still terribly painful to discuss."

"I'm sorry, Mr. Samuels," I said. "I did not mean to stir up these emotions in you, truly. All I am hoping to do is learn the truth about what happened. So...as troubling as it is, I must hear if there was anyone, anyone at all you can think of, who might have done this to her."

Mr. Samuels took a long moment to consider. "I still can think of no one," he said. "And in these circumstances, I would happily point blame at anyone who even looked at her wrong." He shook his head. "But there is no one. She was courted by one young man, who I believe intended to propose before the winter was over. She had few friends, but those she had are as devastated as we are. As for those she danced with...she never sought the lead roles, always those in the background. There would never have been reason to target her, as timid as she was..."

This was all going nowhere, and fast. One victim with no history or connections to speak of, and another with no blemish or fault to speak of. How was I going to find Nightmare if he continued to choose victims who would make it nigh impossible to find him?

I tried not to dwell on the thought that this might be the very reason he chose them in the first place.

"Miss Crawford, I am sorry, but I can give you no further information, apart from a list of those she was closest to. I know nothing of this Nightmare or this Sergeant McCoy. Speaking with us any further will not suddenly make us recall anything about them, either."

"I understand," I said.

"And this is all far more difficult to speak of than I ever imagined it could be..." he said, his voice trailing off. "I must...I cannot – "

"It's quite all right, Mr. Samuels," Eugene said. "We will not ask any more of you. We know how difficult this must be, and so we will not push you any further." He glanced at me.

"Of course," I agreed, seeing the glint in Eugene's gaze. "We would never want to ask more of you than you could give. We appreciate your willingness to speak with us."

Mr. Samuels did not look terribly pleased. "Yes, well...

I wish more than anything that I did have something to share."

"If we have any further questions, might we stop by once more and speak with you?" Eugene asked.

"Yes," Mr. Samuels said. "Of course."

He walked Eugene and me to the front door, where we found Ronald standing out by the car, waiting patiently for us.

"I am going to find who did this to your daughter, Mr. Samuels," I said, turning to him. "I assure you."

Mr. Samuels pursed his lips in a tight, disbelieving smile. "I would be grateful if you did," he said.

But as Eugene and I walked out to the car, my heart thudded in my chest.

I was already wondering if I could keep my promise.

11

———

"Before you say anything," I said, turning to Eugene as Ronald pulled away from the curb. "I'm sorry for pulling the rug out from underneath you like I did by telling them we are engaged."

Eugene regarded me with a curious look. "I understand why you said what you did," he replied. "Though it surprised me that you chose to pretend. That seemed an unnecessary bit of information, didn't it?"

My cheeks colored, and I looked away. "I – Well, I suppose it was, but I thought it would be the most convincing explanation as to why you were working with me, wouldn't it?"

Ronald chuckled in the front seat, and I shot a glare at the back of his neck.

I groaned, pounding my fist against my knee. "We have nothing, still. Nothing! And our time is growing short."

"We still have enough time," Eugene said. "Maybe if

we went back to the theater, we could look around a bit more."

I chewed on the inside of my lip. It was a possibility, but it felt like a waste of time.

"No..." I said a few moments later. "I think we need to look at this differently."

"How?" Eugene asked.

"I'm not quite sure yet..." I said.

"Miss, if I may?" Ronald asked, glancing over his shoulder at me. "Would it be wise to now seek the help of others?"

"Others?" I asked. "Who?"

"Well...perhaps it's time we go back to the authorities," he said. "You told them there would be another death, and they doubted you. You ended up being right, though. They cannot deny that."

I looked at Eugene.

"He has a point, you know," Eugene said. "Maybe we should head straight there and demand to speak with one of the detectives. Maybe Ronald's right; it could very well be time to bring in others to help share this burden."

"Many hands make light work, and all that," Ronald added with a nod of his head.

"Right," Eugene said. "And who knows? Maybe they will have a greater means of helping us, allowing us to solve this tonight before anyone else gets hurt."

I considered for a moment. A doubt crept to the surface, reminding me of the first rule that Nightmare had laid out for us. "He did say we would be allowed to go the police for assistance..." I said. "But he also said it wouldn't help."

"That could be him playing tricks with your mind, Miss," Ronald said. "Sewing seeds of doubt."

"It's clever, really," Eugene said. "If he can make you second guess yourself, then he will have already won half the battle."

I frowned. "Maybe we are in way over our heads right now," I murmured. I nodded. "All right, I think you are both right. It's time to stop allowing my stubbornness to have any authority in this matter. We should go see what we can do."

"Very good, Miss," Ronald said, and took a hard right at the next intersection.

He took us to the nearest station. It was not the largest in the city, but it was located in one of the wealthier neighborhoods, and as such was bigger than some of the others. Ronald explained a bit about the history of the neighborhood to us as we drove, but I imagined it was nothing more than to fill the silence in the air, muffling some of the apprehension hanging over us.

"I NEED to speak with the lead detective on your latest murder case," I announced.

With a snort, the officer's eyes narrowed. "Who do you think you are? Coming in here with such a ridiculous demand?"

"We are private investigators," Eugene said, stepping up to the desk. "And you, sir, have no reason to be so terribly rude to the lady."

The officer slammed down his pen. "I have no reason to act any particular way to those who come in here thinking they can just speak to whomever they wish!" he snapped. "I – "

"Clarkson?"

A door behind him swung open, and a round faced man with a snowy white moustache poked his head out, glaring at the younger man at the desk.

"Yes, sir?" said the officer, his face flushing crimson, before spinning around in his seat to grin ingratiatingly at the man. "I – I did not mean to disturb you, of course, just trying to ask these people to move on and quit bothering – "

"What did they need?" the man with the mustache asked, stepping partly out the door, eyeing us with some interest.

"I – Well, they *wanted* to see you, which I told them was strictly out of the question," the officer said, shaking his head.

The older man looked at us, his wide forehead wrinkling. "And why did you wish to see me specifically?" he asked. "Hardly anyone ever asks to see me particularly."

"They claim to be private investigators, sir," the officer began, nervously shifting and stacking loose papers on his desk.

"Private investigators, you say?" the man asked, showing a spark of interest. "Why, I hardly ever have the chance to meet professionals outside the force. Yes, why don't you come in?"

"But sir, we do not know these people," exclaimed the officer, jumping to his feet. "What if they are not who they say?"

"Settle down, man," the detective said, glaring at the officer. "You need to control yourself. If you keep steering people in need of assistance away, I might have no choice but to reassign you elsewhere."

The officer spun his chair around and sat himself down in it once more. "Of course, sir," he sputtered. "I'm terribly sorry, sir."

The detective shook his head, and stepped aside, gesturing us to follow him into the room beyond. I didn't stop to wait, looking behind me for just a moment at the officer, who harrumphed in his seat.

"There we are," the detective said, closing the door behind us.

We found ourselves in a rather handsome corner office with windows in both the southern and western walls. A desk, cluttered and unorganized was the center-piece of the room, with hardly any other furniture to speak of.

"I apologize for the mess. I transferred here about two weeks ago, and still haven't unpacked entirely," he said with a laugh. "The name's Benedict. Detective Benedict Weatherby. Don't worry too much about the chap out there. He's as tightly wound as a wasp some days."

He scooped up a coat and a pile of books from the nearest chair, and with the tip of his boot, straightened it to face his desk. "For you here, Miss," he said, dumping his armful into another chair beside the door.

I took the seat, Eugene coming to stand beside me.

"I am sorry to say that I didn't quite catch your names," Mr. Weatherby said, eyeing us both.

"We didn't give them," Eugene said. "I am Mr. Osbourn, and this is Miss Crawford. To be perfectly plain, sir, she is the private detective, she and her brother. I am simply filling in for him in his absence."

No sense in telling him that my brother's absence was permanent, was there?

"Miss Crawford?" Mr. Weatherby's eyes widened, his mouth falling open beneath his bristly moustache in surprise. "I have been hoping for the chance to meet you."

"Is that so?" I asked.

"It certainly is," Mr. Weatherby said. "I was most impressed with the story I read in the paper about your handling of the death of Mr. Culpepper."

"It seems that is the case many hear about," I said.

"As prominent a family as the Burkes? Well, it certainly makes sense," he said. "Well, then, what can I do for you?"

"I am here to ask for your help on a case that I am currently working on...and I hate to be the bearer of bad news, but time is greatly of the essence."

"I see," he said, folding his hands.

I began to explain the situation, and before I knew it, I was going into greater and greater detail than I had ever intended. The moment I realized he was listening to what I had to say, I took it as permission to continue. When he did not stop me, I took the chance.

"Well, now..." Mr. Weatherby said, sitting back in his seat. "That is interesting, isn't it?"

Interesting...and terrifying.

"Do you have those letters you were talking about?" he asked.

I pulled them free from my satchel, setting them on the desk between us.

He picked them up, and silently pieced through them, his eyes narrowing further with every word he read. "This is concerning..." he said, sighing heavily. "And this has all occurred within the past few days?"

"Yes, sir," I said. I looked around the room and spotted a clock sitting atop his shelf. "And we only have a few more hours before another death occurs."

He nodded, and I was grateful that he did not speculate that this might not happen.

"Are there any more letters?" he asked.

"No," I said. "Just these."

"He didn't leave one with the most recent victim?"

"No," I said. "Which I found strange as well."

"He sent the letter ahead of time," Eugene said. "Letting us know to keep our eye on the newspaper. That's how we found her."

"So, there is no hint as to where the next murder might occur?" he asked.

"The only possible clue we have is the proximity of the deaths," Eugene said. "The other two deaths occurred within a few miles of one another. We have no proof that the same might happen with this one, but it is possible."

"Possible, and probable," Mr. Weatherly said with a nod. "If only there had been some other indication of where he intended to strike next..." His gaze sharpened. "And you have no idea of who this could be? Anyone from your past? Or an enemy from one of your previous cases?"

"We have spent some time discussing that very matter," I said. "And the only person we could think capable, well, we went to visit him in prison today. It wasn't him."

"You're positive?" Mr. Weatherby asked. "These men

are keen liars, and have fooled even me, and I have been doing this for nigh thirty years."

"I – " I hesitated, wondering if I might have been fooled entirely by Mr. Ward.

"He wasn't lying," Eugene said. "He was perfectly clear that he had no reason to associate with people like Sergeant McCoy, no need for mercenaries. He also laughed when we gave Nightmare's name."

"Well, of course he would have," Mr. Weatherby said.

"Yes, but if it was him who hired a killer to accomplish these murders on the outside, there isn't a great deal that I could do about it; he's already in prison," I said.

"Exactly," Mr. Weatherby said. "And he could torment you all he wanted from there."

"I am not convinced," Eugene said. "Miss Crawford is quite proficient at knowing when someone is lying."

Mr. Weatherby shrugged. "Very well," he said. "All I am saying is that it is not wise to dismiss anyone. Not yet."

"I hear what you are saying," I said. "And I will certainly take it into consideration."

"So allow me to reflect for a moment," he said. "You have no further letters, no idea where the next death might occur, and no idea who might be in danger. Is this correct?"

I licked my lips, resisting the urge to grind my teeth. "Yes."

"Well, then I believe I am going to tell you something you already know. I have some influence over the other departments here, but we simply cannot have every part of this city patrolled, and there would be no way to confirm a murder unless it actually happens."

"So you won't do anything?" I asked. "You'll just let someone die?"

"We cannot predict the future, you or I," he said, quite plainly. "I'm sorry. I appreciate what you are doing, and the challenge you face. I will send men out tonight, to keep an eye on some of the more unsavory areas. However, I cannot promise you anything."

I looked down, my fingers knotted so tightly together they were as white as the bone beneath. "I understand," I said. "And thank you for your time."

There was no reason to argue. There was nothing that could be done.

As we stepped into Richard's house some time later, I heard the chime of midnight...and stopped in my tracks.

I listened to all twelve chimes, my heart slamming against my ribs.

I braced myself, and Eugene reached out to lay a hand on my shoulder.

A death was happening somewhere in the city, right that very moment...and it was entirely my fault.

12

I informed everyone in the house that I intended to wait for the inevitable letter from Nightmare. No one argued with me, giving me space as I settled myself down in a chair near the door in the foyer. It seemed by the time we got home, all three of my cousins had gone to bed. Richard had remained awake, as had Hughes.

"What can I get for you, Miss?" Hughes asked as I settled in.

I sighed, shaking my head. My mind, gummed up with cobwebs, had little motivation to think. "I don't know," I said finally. "Something warm."

Hughes shifted his gaze to Eugene, who had pulled up a chair beside my own. "And you, sir?"

"Whatever you find for her," he said. "Thank you."

"Certainly," Hughes said, and departed from us.

Richard stepped up, bending down to squat beside my chair. "You look dreadful," he said, a wry smirk fixing to his face that, at the moment, reminded me so much of my brother Felix.

I rolled my eyes, looking away. "Well aren't you kind?"

"It might be time to put this investigation to bed, Lillian," Richard said. "With each passing moment, it seems more fruitless – "

"And yet, because of my inability to learn the truth, it is likely a third person has died," I said.

"Remember, that Sergeant was already dead when the first letter arrived for you," Richard said, folding his hands between his knees. "You must stop taking responsibility for that one."

I groaned, letting my head fall back against the tufted seat.

Richard asked about what we had learned, and Eugene mercifully gave the account in my stead. I closed my eyes, willing the throbbing in my head to cease, when their words became distant, and tangled.

Before I knew it, my head snapped up once again, and I found myself in complete darkness.

The gentle rumble beside me drew my eye, and I found the silhouette of Eugene asleep in the chair beside me. His head lay back against the seat, and one arm had slipped off the armrest and hung limply at his side.

I blinked a few times, rubbing the sleep from my eyes, and massaging the tense muscles in my neck. How long had I slept?

Slowly, I stood and stretched my aching limbs, and walked over to the large window beside the front door.

The first grey light of dawn scored the horizon, like the stroke of a paintbrush. I stared at it, my heart sinking. Nothing had happened during the night but that gave me no peace. I knew deep down that another murder had occurred, and I had once again been powerless to stop it.

I wandered to the door, and after fiddling with the locks for a moment, pulled it open. I half expected a letter to be waiting on the threshold, but saw nothing. Cold air rushed in, chilling my very bones.

I closed the door and locked it once more, before leaning against it.

My eyes itched from lack of enough sleep, and my stomach grumbled. I wondered if I had eaten a proper meal in three days. My back ached just between my shoulder blades, and the knots in my chest had only faded to a dull ache as I'd slept. Now that I was awake, they burned and twisted with renewed vigor.

What was I supposed to do? How was I going to solve this?

"Lillian?"

I heard Eugene's quiet voice through the darkness, and despite the chill, it warmed my heart ever so slightly.

He appeared a moment later, coming to stand with me at the window. With squinting eyes and a stifled yawn he regarded me, massaging the wrist of his hand that had hung limply beside him; I assumed it prickled with numbness. "Is everything all right?"

"I hardly know," I murmured. "There has been no news yet."

He nodded, exhaling heavily through his nostrils. "And yet you expect some, I assume?"

"How could I not?" I asked.

Eugene licked his lips. "Perhaps he has given up."

"That's an idle fantasy," I said.

"We don't know that," he said.

"I do..." I said softly.

He said nothing for a moment, then reached out and slipped my hand into his. "I realize we face a great deal of uncertainty," he whispered. "But I assure you I will remain at your side no matter what comes, all right?"

I nodded, and pinched my eyelids shut for a brief moment. "I'm just so tired..." I muttered.

Eugene convinced me to sit down for breakfast with the rest of my family, which was not terribly difficult to do, as hungry as I was. While I devoured several poached eggs, ham, and some delicious apple tarts, I listened to the normal humdrum conversation between Gloria, Marie, Richard and William. I indulged myself for a moment, allowing myself to believe life was not as dark and treacherous as it really was, and that my greatest concerns could also revolve around Marie's wedding which was so quickly approaching. In truth, I'd hardly thought of it in the past few days.

When Hughes entered the room, however, looking grim, I regretted the bountiful meal I'd partaken in.

My insides churned as his gaze fell upon me, and he held up a letter.

I glared at it as the room fell silent, watching as he brought it to me.

"I might come to hate the very sight of the post once all this is through," I said through gritted teeth, tearing the parchment open.

Once again, the letter was short.

See today's paper. You'll notice a small story about a man named Mr. Simeon Bertram, a banker of great influence. Quite wealthy and well-liked by those in the community, he made the unfortunate mistake of walking home on his own late last evening. Oh, dear...if only he had taken the time to do his shopping earlier in the day. Such a pity.

I am beginning to think you are losing your touch, Miss Crawford, but don't give up. This will continue until you have solved it!

Kindest Regards.

My hand crumpled around the letter.

"What does it say?" Eugene asked.

I tossed it on the table, pushing my chair back with a *screech* of the legs. "Richard, I need that paper – " I said, striding to the head of the table and snatching the newspaper right out of his hand.

As Eugene read the letter aloud to those at the table, I quickly paged through the paper until I stumbled upon the name Nightmare had suggested in the letter.

"It's true..." I said, my head swimming. "Right here."

"Does it say where he was?" Eugene asked.

"Yes," I said, and laying the paper down, I tore the article out with swift if uneven rips, leaving the rest for him. "Let's go."

Eugene and I wasted no more time, sending for Ronald as soon as he could ready himself. We were on the road within the next twenty minutes, and reached the site of the death within the hour.

The road had been blocked off, and police vehicles lined the streets to prevent passersby from wandering down. It was by no means a main drag, but it seemed to be causing a great deal of consternation to the local populace who likely used that thoroughfare every day for work and other daily activities.

"Ronald, pull right up to where those officers are," I said. "We will likely need to get permission to enter here."

"Certainly," he said, and did as I asked.

Eugene walked with me right to the officers, who seemed to hardly take notice of us as we approached.

"Excuse me?" I asked. "My name is Lillian Crawford, and I am a private detective. This Mr. Bertram? Yes, he is part of my case."

The four officers gathered together all turned to look at us. The one closest to me, with hair as blonde as wheat, stared. "Miss Crawford? From the Culpepper and Lee murders?"

"The same," I said. "Now, if you might be so kind, time is of the essence, and I must see this Mr. Bertram."

"I'm sorry, Miss, but we have been ordered not to allow anyone past," said a younger officer without a great deal of confidence, pointing over his shoulder.

"Yes, but I have spoken with your superiors about this matter within the past few days. Do any of you work with a Detective Weatherby?" I asked.

The blonde officer eyed the wiry officer beside him apprehensively. "Yes, we do," he said. "But – "

"He is well aware of my case, and if you wish to discuss this matter any further, I suggest you take it up with him," I said, pushing past them to stride between two of the cars blocking the road.

I heard protests behind me, but ignored them as Eugene and I walked onto the scene.

Only a portion of the road had been blocked, but it seemed obvious why after we caught sight of the body.

Mr. Bertram lay sprawled in the middle of the road, his arms and legs stretched out on both sides. He wore a dark suit, but the white of his shirt had been stained crimson, and a trail of blood ran from beneath him all the way to the sewer grate in the road.

"Bullet wound," Eugene said darkly as we approached.

He was right; his suit coat lay open, revealing a black, silk vest with a perfect hole right where his heart lay. The blood having seeped into the vest around the wound had leached the shine from the fabric, ruining it.

"It looks like he fell backwards..." I murmured, trying to avoid looking directly at the hole in his chest, as small as it was. "As if he were startled."

"I imagine he was killed instantly," Eugene said, also in a low voice. "Or nearly so."

I looked around. "Do you see a letter?"

He and I took a few moments to look, but I already knew the answer before we had begun to look. No, there were no more letters.

He really doesn't want to make this easy on us, does he?

"Killed right out in the open..." Eugene said, looking around. "On a rather well traveled street, too. Nightmare is growing bolder."

Goosebumps raced up my arms. "Which isn't exactly encouraging to hear."

"Well, this means he is taking higher risks, which likely means more mistakes," Eugene said.

"Perhaps," I said.

I noticed an array of boxes nearby, all scattered around as if they'd been thrown. My eyes narrowed as I looked at them, and then back to Mr. Bertram. "Are these his?" I wondered, heading over to them.

They were lovely, wrapped in delicate, colorful paper and tied up with golden ribbons. A card lay beside one of the larger boxes, with a simple *Happy Birthday* written across it. I turned it over, but saw nothing more.

We pulled one of the policemen over and asked about the boxes.

"We have no idea," he said. "We assume they belonged to Mr. Bertram, as close as they were to him. And he seemed to be coming from the direction of some shops that offer the same sort of wrapping services as these appear to be."

"But you don't know if they are his? Or what's in them?" I asked.

He shook his head.

I eyed them warily. If they did belong to him, then it was possible Nightmare would have used them to hide something. "For the sake of the investigation, we need to open them," I told Eugene.

He gave me a firm nod, and we began to unwrap them, one by one.

We found a train set, a doll, and a series of books for children. My insides twisted. These were likely for his own child...but now they would never arrive.

"I wonder if he knew the Samuels?" I asked. "What connection might be there?"

"I suppose we would have to ask," Eugene said. "Both victims do appear to be from families of means..."

I still did not understand how his death tied in with the Sergeant's, however. "And all three of them have died in entirely different ways," I said. "So it isn't as if we can garner anything from how these people all died. There was nothing to connect them together in that regard."

"No, but would that really have given us any clues?" Eugene asked.

I shrugged. "Perhaps. If it was the same weapon, then maybe we could track down whoever made it, and then find any number of buyers – " I stopped, my heart sinking. "But that doesn't matter, does it? This whole conversation doesn't matter – this whole *thing* is out of control."

"Lillian, you must calm yourself," Eugene said. "We will not be able to solve this otherwise."

I looked over at Mr. Bertram, and then at a pair of policemen walking toward him with a black tarp carried between them. My heart skipped, and I hurried toward them. "Wait! I haven't finished examining – "

"Sorry, Miss, but these are our orders," said the officer I noticed to be the same blonde officer we met when we arrived on the scene. "We have to get this street opened up. It's been too long already."

"I just need a few more minutes," I said, quickly staring at every inch of the victim's suit that I could, at the wound, at his tie – anything that could give me a clue.

"I'm sorry," the policeman said, frowning as he helped to drape the tarp over the body. "This is all we can do."

I had no choice but to step back and allow them to wrap up the body. Eugene stood beside me, trying to usher me away. "Let's go back to Ronald," he said in a low voice. "We need to go."

I reluctantly let him pull me away, back toward the car. I tried not to allow distress to press in all around me, threatening to engulf me.

We climbed into the back of the car, and Ronald pulled away from the curb with a reluctant look at me over his shoulder.

"Each death leaves me with more questions," I said. "I had even less time to look at this victim than I did the ballerina." I groaned. "This whole thing...there has to be a pattern, right? Otherwise I will never be able to find out who did this."

"That's true," Eugene said. "If the killer is playing a game, then there have to be some rules."

"You would certainly think so," I said, crossing my arms. "Except when he doesn't seem to be playing by them! There don't seem to be *any* rules at all!"

My head collapsed back against the seat, and I grimaced. "I looked at everything I could, and saw nothing, *nothing* that would even suggest this was done by Nightmare. All I have to go by is his ridiculous letter!"

"I am in complete agreement with you that there must be something that ties them all together, more than just what we have seen in the letters," Eugene said. "We still have some time during the day, we can still work this out – "

"Will time change anything we know?" I asked. "No, it won't. We can't examine the bodies, we can't find anything from the letters, it's...it's almost hopeless."

Eugene could find nothing to say, sighing, shaking his head.

I turned to stare out the window, frowning. "I am beginning to wonder if I am not playing a game, so much as being played with."

13

W e did our due diligence and went to the home of Mr. Bertram, but found his family to be even less helpful than Mr. Samuels had been. They had no recollection of Miss Samuels, and were offended when we insinuated they had any connection to a mercenary. They chased us out before a quarter of an hour passed. Not that it mattered. I had expected no new information, and found precisely that.

We arrived back at Richard's, as I could not come up with a single other place that might be worth going to afterward.

"We could go back to Detective Weatherby," Eugene suggested from his place at the dinner table. At Hughes suggestion, we had set it up as a bit of a command station where we might review the information we had. Not that we had much, of course, but it made me feel better to have more minds than my own working on this.

"No," I said, shaking my head, laying my hands flat on the table. The letters were spread out in order before me.

I had read them a dozen times, at least. "Weatherby couldn't do anything."

"Why not?" Richard asked. "The situation has changed since you saw him yesterday."

"Yes, it happened just as I said it would," I said, shooting him a glare down the table. "He didn't want to listen to me."

"I don't think it's that he didn't want to listen," Eugene said. "There was just nothing much he could do at the time, was there? Not when he couldn't have predicted when or how someone would be killed."

"But now we know more," I realized. "So yes, maybe there would be more information to give, things he would know something about that we don't."

Richard looked at Hughes. "Would you telephone the police station and ask if this Mr. Weatherby could pay us a visit?" he asked.

Hughes bowed his head. "Right away."

My spirits rose, and I felt slightly more confident. I had little reason to believe Weatherby *could* help, but knew he would at least be willing.

I glanced up at the makeshift board Hughes had brought in earlier, made of an old door draped with a linen cloth used only for moving furniture. We had pinned some newspaper clippings to it, along with a map of downtown London that Richard had found in his desk. The radius around the deaths had been circled in red ink, with three pins in each of the places where the bodies had been found.

"The only thing that seems to make any sense is the location of death," I muttered, walking up to the map. "But something else must tie them together. Surely."

"I imagine it must," Richard said, joining me.

"Even if it is not readily apparent," Eugene added, coming to stand beside me as well. "And there was nothing in the newspaper articles? No mention of any of the other names?"

"No," I said, sighing.

"Well, then we must address the possibility that some of the people you have spoken with are lying to you," Richard said, folding his arms, staring at the map with a wrinkled brow.

"And that they really are connected in some way..." I said. "What if Mr. Bertram was having an affair with the ballerina? Or what if he hired the mercenary for some nefarious purpose?"

"The trouble with those possibilities is that it is unlikely his family would have known," Richard said, frowning. "Those truths would have died with him."

"Or what if the ballerina was related to the mercenary some way that the family did not realize?" I asked. "What if the wife had an affair and the ballerina was, in fact, not Mr. Samuels' daughter at all?"

"Then what of the banker? How does he fit in?" Eugene asked.

I groaned, sinking down into one of the dining chairs. "This is hopeless!"

I rubbed my temples, feeling strangely vulnerable, empty.

I know what it is. I wish Felix were here. He would surely see this from a way that I simply cannot.

I got to my feet, striding toward the door.

"Where are you going?" Eugene asked.

"To write a letter to Felix," I said over my shoulder.

"Is that wise right now?" Richard called after me.

I whirled around. "It will help me think. I...I need a few moments alone to try and get my thoughts in order."

Eugene and Richard exchanged a concerned look.

"I won't be long," I said.

"Lillian, a letter will not arrive in New York before – " Eugene said.

"Yes, before there is a pile of bodies, I know," I snapped. "But it will help me think, even if I never actually send it."

I didn't wait for another argument before I swept out of the room.

I headed to Richard's study, knowing I would find the paper I needed there. I didn't want to linger to catch whatever snippets of conversation Richard and Eugene might have. I passed through the foyer, and found Hughes standing at the door with Oswald.

"Good evening," Oswald said, his eyes alight with surprise. "Is – "

"She's upstairs," I said, not stopping.

"No, I meant Eugene," he called after me as I made my way into the next hallway.

"Dining room," I said.

I found the paper and pen I needed, and started back to the dining room.

As I headed back, voices in the foyer gave me pause. It was Oswald and Eugene, and they were speaking in hushed tones.

"...do not need to trouble her with this right now," Oswald said. "You know that. It wouldn't be wise."

"I do not think I should keep this from her," Eugene

argued in a whisper. "Obviously there is nothing any of us can do, but – "

"That's precisely my point," Oswald countered. "There is nothing anyone can do. They'll find her eventually."

I moved toward the wall, and with muffled footsteps, inched toward the open archway into the foyer. I leaned against the wall, and listened closely.

The only "her" I could think of that Oswald might be referring to was me. He wanted Eugene to keep something from me. What could that possibly be?

The idea that he was sneaking around, hiding something from me, unsettled me.

"Where was she last seen?" Eugene asked.

"The asylum," Oswald said with frustration. "The police seem to be several steps behind her."

A cold, terrible chill washed over me.

Asylum? That could only mean –

"And they have no idea where she could have gone?" Eugene asked.

"The only places they have checked are places we suggested," Oswald said, and I heard the *clap* of his hands falling to his sides.

"And there was no sign of her?" Eugene asked.

There was no response, but I imagined Oswald shaking his head.

Eliza. It has to be!

"Why did you feel the need to come all the way out here to tell me?" Eugene asked. "We knew she had escaped. Did something happen?"

"No, and that's the trouble, isn't it?" Oswald said. "Father went to the asylum to speak with the security, and they said it baffled them how she managed to escape. It's almost as if she walked out through the front doors."

"How?" Eugene asked.

"They don't know," Oswald answered. "They assume she found a uniform of one of the nurses, or perhaps just put on ordinary clothes, impersonating a visitor."

"I don't understand how they could have been so lax..." Eugene murmured. He sighed. "What in the world is she doing? Where is she?"

"That's what worries Father, given what happened before," Oswald said. "Her escape seemed well planned and thorough. And the note she left for the head doctor made it seem as if she thought it laughable, how they had tried to constrain her."

Another chill raced down my back. It had been some time since we had confronted Eliza, finding that she had been the one to kill one of Oswald's brother's friends, Mr. Dossett. It had been different than the other cases I had investigated. This one had been personally tied to Eugene, involving his family. In the end, Felix and I had discovered that Eugene's own cousin had been the killer.

I still lost sleep over that encounter. Eliza had legitimately lost her mind, lost all sense of herself. For the safety of the general public, the authorities had placed her in an asylum for the criminally insane. And yet –

"It can't be anything good, whatever she is up to," Oswald went on.

That much was certain.

I gasped, clapping my hand over my mouth.

I knew. Suddenly, I knew.

Nightmare...Eliza...

They were one and the same.

My heart thundered in my chest, making me dizzy. I pressed myself up against the wall, my knees trembling as the pieces slid into place like heavy, iron keys in their matching locks.

Memories flashed across my mind of the girl, her wicked glances, her keen intellect. Nightmare, likewise, had seemed cleverer than the average murderer. He – or she, really – had covered her tracks well, leaving no trace, no clue –

But how? How could I be certain? I couldn't go on a hunch, could I?

No...I knew. I knew exactly what it was.

"Ribbons!" I shrieked, hurrying out from around the corner.

Eugene and Oswald both leapt away from me, looking startled.

"Lillian!" Eugene exclaimed. "What are you – "

I ran to him, grabbing his forearms, my eyes fixed upon his as I squeezed him for dear life. "Eugene, it's the ribbons! How did I not see it before?"

"Ribbons?" Oswald asked. "What are you talking about?"

"Each death, each victim – ribbons – they were there, at every single one!" I exclaimed.

Eugene's eyes searched my face until they lit up with understanding. "The ribbons..." he murmured, and I could see the same revelation filling his mind.

"You're mad, the both of you," Oswald said, taking a wary step away from us.

"Sergeant McCoy," I said, my mind working far faster than my mouth would cooperate. "We saw the flowers! The ribbon was tied around the flowers!"

"And the ballerina," Eugene added, nodding fervently. "The white ribbon in her hair and tied in her dance shoes."

"The packages!" I exclaimed. "Mr. Bertram's packages were tied up in gold ribbons!"

Oswald stared back and forth between us. "I don't understand – "

I rounded on him. "Eliza strangled Mr. Dossett with a ribbon, the same kind she always wore in her hair. *That* was the clue we have been missing!"

Eugene clapped his hands together. "That's it! It must be!" Then the realization of his words, the real truth, settled over him, for he looked suddenly horrified. "That means Eliza is Nightmare."

Oswald gaped at me. "You aren't serious?"

"When was she reported missing?" I asked, moving to stand before him.

He took a wary step backward. "A few days ago, I believe."

"The first letter that arrived came around the same time," Eugene said, scratching his chin. "Very close to it."

"And the police haven't been able to find her?" I asked Oswald.

"No," he said.

"Have they caught sight of her, at all?" I asked.

"No," he repeated. "Not once."

I looked at Eugene. "We did. We should have known it was a woman when she jumped off the roof."

"We did notice she was much shorter than we had expected," Eugene said.

"Wait, she jumped off a building?" Oswald asked, his brows shooting up toward his hairline.

We didn't have time to waste. Not now.

"She's mad," I said. "This twisted game could only come out of the mind of a lunatic with a vendetta against me."

"And she would be clever enough to invent it," Eugene said. "Without a doubt."

"You are suggesting she broke out of the asylum so she could torment you and kill people?" Oswald asked, his expression hardening. "That seems so...so – "

"Insane?" I asked. "Yes, well, this is the sanest I have felt in the past seventy-two hours."

"It's her," Eugene agreed. "It has to be."

"We have to move," I said, turning to hurry toward the dining room.

"Wait," Eugene said. "Where are we going to go?"

"I don't know," I said, my heart hammering against my ribs. "But we know the truth. That means we are that much closer to finding her."

14

This might not have been the most thought out plan I had ever concocted, but given the shortness of time, it was the best we could do.

I stood in a pool of light, cast from a streetlamp much the same as the others that lined the streets on both sides. The hour was late enough that hardly a soul had been seen. That was good. It was what we had counted on in the first place.

My hand trembled slightly, but it wasn't the gun in my hand, slick with sweat, that worried me. It was unloaded; a ploy and nothing more. No, it was the realization that these could very well be the last few moments of my life, regardless of the fact I was only pretending to want to take my own life.

It was strange to realize it had only been a few hours since the whole family, including Oswald, Eugene, and I had sat down at the dining room table together to work out a plan. I knew we would have to do something to lure Eliza out into the open. Eugene agreed with at least that much – she had revealed herself at the theater, whether willingly or not, and so, we knew she had to be watching us.

"The only way will be to anger her enough," Oswald said, shaking his head. "That seems to be the only thing she really ever responded to."

"That, or corner her somehow, so she feels vulnerable, pushing her to try and attack," Eugene said.

We went back and forth for some time before I came up with an idea. I knew she would smell a setup as soon as she saw it, so we would need to make it convincing, which would mean taking some risks.

"No," Eugene had said, even before Richard did. He shook his head firmly. "Absolutely not. I will not allow this."

"Can you think of another way?" I countered.

Silence greeted my remark, and no one seemed to be able to come up with anything better or safer.

And so, I found myself standing in the middle of the street, about half a mile from the cemetery where this had all begun...with an empty gun clutched tightly in my hand.

I knew we didn't have a great deal of time. The eleventh hour had already come, and dwindled away with each passing second. I knew we only had our hunches to go on, but they told us Eliza would more likely want to follow us and see what we were up to, instead of pursuing another target. This would be the first time in four nights that we were out actively looking for her near midnight. We hoped she would be curious enough to keep tabs on us.

Our entire plan hinged on it.

Eugene and Richard were nearby, waiting in one of the buildings where one of Richard's friends lived. They would see if anything went awry. Whether they could reach me in time was another story.

I steeled myself, and knew I was just wasting time, standing in the middle of the street like I was.

I drew in a deep breath, hand still shaking as I raised the gun.

I flinched as the cold metal kissed the skin of my temple, my eyes slamming shut. It wasn't loaded. I was safe, but that didn't mean this didn't feel like an incredibly stupid thing to be doing.

"I – I can't do this anymore!" I wailed into the darkness, my voice hitching. I swallowed, my throat dry. "You've won, Nightmare! I can't be responsible for any more deaths!"

I hoped my yelling wasn't enough to draw attention from the wrong sort. I really only wanted Eliza.

"This...this has to end, one way or another!" I cried.

"No, no, no..."

My heart skipped several times as the voice reached me. I whipped around, and saw Eliza swaggering toward me from an unknown location, her black hood lowered. Until this moment, she might have been sitting on the steps of the nearest house, for all I knew. I could be sure it was her, though, not only by her voice, but by seeing her astonishingly pretty face and her fiery copper hair...tied in a crimson silk ribbon.

"This isn't how this is supposed to end, Lillian dear," she said, folding her arms. Every part of her body had been clothed in black, from the tips of her fingers, all the way to the ends of her toes. Leather boots, black trousers, black cloak, black leather gloves.

She cocked her hip, tilting her head as she stared at me. "You can't just give up!"

Now that she was standing in front of me, I had absolutely no idea what to do, what to say. It astonished me that we had been right. We had guessed this would draw her in, and here she stood in front of me, tapping her foot, glaring at me just like she always did.

I didn't know how to begin.

She was so close I could have just reached out and grabbed her. It would have been easy to grab hold of the front of her cloak, drag her to the ground and pin her there until Eugene and Richard could reach us. I could have taken hold of that loose braid of hers, swaying in the wind, and forced her to her knees.

Instead, I smirked...and turned the pistol away from my own head, pointing it straight at her heart.

Eliza's eyes lit up as she stared down the barrel.

Her face split open like a gaping wound, far too wide, and she *laughed* at me.

Did she know? How could she have known?

My heart thundered in my chest, even more than it had when I had been pointing the pistol at myself. Some words Richard had once spoken what seemed like an eternity ago drifted back through my mind.

You will only see that *form of yourself again when the danger is so great it has no other choice but to appear.*

He had been talking about how troubled I was after nearly killing Mr. Ward...and how easily I would have actually done so in that moment. I had been protecting myself, protecting Felix and all the others in the room, but I would have killed someone.

And yet...here I stood, knowing full well how this encounter was likely to end. I knew it had to be me that took action. It was me she was targeting, after all.

Would I have the courage? Would that part of me show up, just like Richard had said it would? Though I was terrified of that part of myself and of the chance to see it once again, I was even more frightened of what havoc Eliza could cause.

How far would she go without me standing in her way?

"Oh, how *precious* you are," she said, drying her eyes with the tips of her gloved fingers.

"Why are you doing this?" I asked. It was not the most pressing question in my mind, but it spilled out before I could stop it. My voice shook, and all the poise I had hoped to maintain had vanished.

Eliza tossed her braid over her shoulder, surveying the street around her. I noticed her eyes pass from window to window; she had to be looking for anyone else who might have come with me. Eugene, for certain. Maybe even Felix; would she have figured out that he wasn't around, anymore?

"It's simple," Eliza said with a shrug. "Though I created this little challenge to wreak vengeance on you, I discovered that I rather enjoyed it, with the repeated killings. It was fun, really. I had a grand time setting up the bodies and crime scenes for you to examine. Oh, it was a game for me, indeed. Didn't you have any fun? Surely, you must have. The mystery, the intrigue. And it isn't as if any of them were truly important people anyway. Society will hardly miss them..." She started to walk around me. I didn't dare lower the gun, but followed her in the tight circle she walked.

"I assume you targeted me because I landed you in the asylum?" I asked.

"Naturally," Eliza said with the flash of a grin. "But I should thank you, really. It helped me to realize my true potential. Those people at the asylum made it too easy for me to escape. It was laughable."

I licked my lips, trying to figure out how to proceed. She was far too comfortable, which made me all the more nervous. What could I do? What *should* I do?

She came to a stop in front of me once again, her eyes meeting mine.

"You won, by the way," she said brightly. "My game. You figured it out. I knew you would. But what is your prize, you might be asking? Well, I have it for you right here."

My heart skipped as she reached beneath her cloak.

Time seemed to slow to a crawl as it flapped out around her like a bat's wing. She withdrew a small pistol, very similar to my own.

I didn't have time to move.

She pointed it at me at the same time I instinctively kicked out with my legs.

In the same moment that my foot slammed into her knee, she pulled the trigger.

15

B*ANG.*

      Three heartbeats passed before I had the courage to look down at my torso. With a trembling hand, I pressed my fingers against my middle...and drew them away slick with warm, red blood.

The pain bloomed in my stomach, first like the kiss of frigid metal, followed by a searing burn like a hot poker. It grew, until a cry escaped my lips as I sank down onto the street, falling to my knees.

Eliza had staggered, caught off guard by my reactionary kick to her knee. She tossed her hair back over her shoulder, straightened again, and stepped closer to me. "Well, it's certainly not what I wanted," she hissed, all traces of friendly teasing gone. "You should be dead. Oh well. It hardly ever works out the way I *really* want it to."

Blackness seeped into the corners of my vision, and I could feel my consciousness slipping. I couldn't collapse now. I had to – had to stay awake –

"Well, I suppose before you do go, I should tell you

where you could have improved," Eliza said. "You were trying so hard to find a pattern, a connection between the victims, when there simply wasn't one at all." She chuckled. "I chose them entirely at random."

If I had any ability to care at the moment, I would have been all the more horrified. I had been right all along; she had simply been playing me like a fiddle.

"I didn't want there to be a pattern," she said. "Or anything that could have tied me to the murders."

I looked up at her. "I...did know..." I barely managed to mutter. "...Your ribbons."

Eliza stopped her pacing, shot me a brief look, but shrugged. "Well, maybe I went a bit *too* poetic with their deaths. Yes, I did leave a ribbon at every scene, and maybe some part of me hoped you would pick up on that – " She let out a bark of a laugh. "Oh, it seems that I am even surprising *myself* with all this! How wonderfully exhilarating, to see that I was perhaps sabotaging myself!"

She twirled around like a gleeful child.

"Yes, I left the ribbon there as my personal nod to you, of course. It makes sense," she said excitedly. Then she spun around again, staring at me. "But that doesn't matter, does it? You didn't figure it out quickly enough, did you? Three people died because you weren't nearly as good at playing detective as you thought you were."

The pain in my torso throbbed and bit. Because of that distraction, her words didn't trouble me as much as she probably hoped.

My head swam, and the whole world spun.

Unable to stop it, I felt my body fall to the side, against the cold, stone street. I welcomed the wet, cool rocks against my cheek, almost a comfort to the raging heat in my middle. I wanted it to stop...I wanted to sleep.

I heard voices, somewhere in the distance outside of my tunneling vision. I blinked a few times, but could barely keep my eyes open.

BANG!

Another gunshot. Somewhere in the back of my mind, I wondered who else Eliza had decided to kill. Was it some unfortunate passerby?

"Eugene!"

My eyes snapped open again, hearing Eliza call his name.

"Drop the gun, Eliza." Eugene's fierce tone drew out life in me again, pushing away some of the darkness. "Now."

"Oh, come now, cousin, you can't really be – "

"I said drop it!" Eugene shouted.

I had one chance. One. And that was if I even had the strength to be able to do it.

Slowly, I reached for the hidden holster around my thigh, where my throwing knives were usually concealed. Not this time, though; I had planned ahead for one last surprise, one last line of defense.

Because I couldn't see Eliza, I assumed she wouldn't be able to see what I was doing either. I moved slowly, partly because I was barely maintaining my hold on consciousness, and partly to avoid detection. Withdrawing the small pistol Richard had loaned me, I rolled onto my back.

Eliza glanced over her shoulder to stare at me, away from Eugene, who had to have been standing somewhere I couldn't quite see.

I smirked at her, raising my hand. "This time, Eliza...it is you who fell for *my* trap..."

And I pulled the trigger.

The bullet struck her square in the back, before she had the chance to turn around. In fact, her movement may have made the wound even more grievous, likely striking her ribcage, and with any success, her heart.

It must have been enough, because she crumpled to the ground like a marionette whose strings had been cut.

My arm collapsed beside me, the gun rolling away.

The darkness threatened me once again, calling to me, welcoming me with open arms.

Brilliant blue eyes swam in my vision, searching my face.

"It's all right, Lillian..." I heard Eugene's voice, but it sounded miles away. "You're safe, now. I'm here."

Good...now I can rest.

With that, I gave way to the darkness, unable to hold on another second longer.

16

"I thought it would be some time before I saw the sea like this again," I said, staring out over the starboard side of the ship. "But I suppose a great deal has happened that I didn't expect, hasn't it?"

Eugene stood beside me, leaning against the railing, staring off into the vast horizon. He turned his gaze upon me, the very same shade of blue as the brilliant sky stretching over our heads. "Indeed," he said. "Though I must admit that this is a desirable turn of events."

I smiled at him. "Again, I'm sorry I balked the way I did at the idea of our wedding happening in New York," I said. "I do believe that will be the best place for it, with our family around."

Eugene glanced over his shoulder, where we could just make out Marie and Oswald sitting on the sun deck chairs together, hand in hand. "I am glad they all agreed to come along."

"I know Richard is perfectly happy for the chance to see my mother again," I said. "They are cousins, after all.

And Felix's letter said he is happy to have them all coming so that he might see them sooner than he had expected."

Eugene nodded.

I eyed him, keenly aware of his thoughts. "Yet you are reminded that there are two people missing from this return voyage...aren't you?"

His smile faltered ever so slightly. "It isn't as if I want them here, not as they were," he said. "I suppose I just wish it had all turned out differently."

I nodded, turning to look out over the sea again.

He shook his head, looking down.

"What is it?" I asked.

"I suppose I am wishing I had managed to propose to you when I tried the first two times."

I blinked at him. "You tried two other times? When?" I asked.

It was his turn to smile. "Well, I first tried when I was to meet you and Felix for lunch in London. Unfortunately, it was the same day he was arrested for murder."

"I remember!" I said. "You shoved something back into your pocket when I hurried into the restaurant to find you."

He nodded, glancing at the ring sparkling on my finger. "That I did. Felix knew of my intentions, though he didn't know precisely when I was to propose."

"Of course he did," I said with a small laugh.

"And the next time was the night we received Eliza's first letter as Nightmare," he said. "I had wanted to take you out for a walk in the gardens and propose there, but when the letter arrived and everything seemed to come crashing down around us..."

"It wasn't the right time," I finished for him.

"Right," he said.

I moved closer to him. "Well, if I can be so honest, I am glad you didn't manage to propose either of those times."

He glanced down at me. "Why? If I had, then maybe we could have prevented some of chaos that happened. If we weren't here, then..." He trailed off.

"We cannot change the past," I said. "And there is no sense worrying over it. Besides, I think the way that you *did* propose was perfect."

A reluctant smile spread across his face. "You do?" he asked. "I thought...well, it didn't happen exactly how I imagined."

I laughed. "How could you have known that William and Gloria would have argued instead of playing the tune you asked them to?" I chuckled. "Well, it is Gloria, I suppose, but that's part of her charm, isn't it?"

He laughed, but shook his head. "And when Hughes misplaced the box the ring was hidden in, I thought I might lose my mind," he said. "Thankfully, *you* found it... but that's not what I had intended."

My heart warmed. "What you intended was to ask me to marry you," I said. "That's what was important."

"Well...then I am happy," he said. "That's all I could have ever hoped for."

He pulled me close to him, and for a while, we allowed the sound of the waves against the ship to be the only thing breaking the silence.

"You're holding your stomach again," Eugene said, stirring me from my thoughts.

I looked down, and he was right.

"Is the wound bothering you?" he asked. "Perhaps it's the rocking of the ship?"

I sighed. "I had hoped that a few months of rest would have me completely healed, but the doctor did say I could have lingering pain and scarring for a long time to come."

Eugene frowned. "I am sorry."

"It isn't your fault," I said, moving my hands away, smiling at him.

I surveyed the sea once again, feeling peace settle over me.

"I think this is the right decision," Eugene said, in a quiet voice. "Leaving England like this."

I nodded. "I couldn't agree more, even if I would have fought you tooth and nail just as I did Felix before everything that happened with Eliza."

Eugene gave me a tight smile. "Yes, well...as we have been saying...everything has not turned out the way we expected."

I leaned against the railing. "I needed to spend some time away from London, though I do want to visit again someday..."

"But for now, you are allowed to enjoy your *own* life, instead of looking out for everyone else's," Eugene said.

I smiled at him. "Yes. For now."

"You have done a great deal of good," he said.

"As have you," I said. "I could not have done it without your help."

He gave me an all too familiar look; he blamed himself partially for my suffering, as it was his sister and his cousin who had inflicted some of the damage.

"I mean that," I said. "For all I know, this would have happened with or without you."

He nodded. "I know. We don't have to go over it again."

"I do look forward to spending some time back in England later, for our honeymoon," I said. "And I think it was wise to schedule several performances for you in London at the same time."

He nodded. "It will be good, I think."

"And we will see what comes of it," I said. "Though I might very well never open another case. I might have had my fill of danger and excitement for the rest of my life."

He laughed softly. "Somehow, I don't quite believe that."

I laughed with him, because I didn't believe it either.

Begin a new series from Blythe Baker with "An Inelegant Death: The Jane Pemberton Murder Mysteries, Book 1."

ABOUT THE AUTHOR

Blythe Baker is the lead writer behind several popular historical and paranormal mystery series. When Blythe isn't buried under clues, suspects, and motives, she's acting as chauffeur to her children and head groomer to her household of beloved pets. She enjoys walking her dogs, lounging in her backyard hammock, and fiddling with graphic design. She also likes binge-watching mystery shows on TV. To learn more about Blythe, visit her website and sign up for her newsletter at www.blythebaker.com

Made in the USA
Columbia, SC
28 March 2023

14449928R00114